PIECES OF ME

Also by Amber Kizer

A Matter of Days
Meridian
Wildcat Fireflies
Speed of Light
Gert Garibaldi's Rants and Raves: One Butt Cheek at a Time
Seven Kinds of Ordinary Catastrophes

PIECES OF ME

AMBER KIZER

DELACORTE PRESS

Text copyright © 2014 by Amber Kizer

Visit us on the Web! randomhouse.com/teens

Educators and librarians, for a variety of teaching tools, visit us at
RHTeachersLibrarians.com

Library of Congress Cataloging-in-Publication Data
Kizer, Amber.
Pieces of me / Amber Kizer. — First edition.
pages cm
Summary: After a car accident leaves her brain-dead, Jessica tries to prevent her parents from donating her organs and tissues, but then follows the lives of four fellow teens who are able to survive because she did not.
ISBN 978-0-385-74116-3 (hc) — ISBN 978-0-375-98429-7 (ebook) —
[1. Donation of organs, tissues, etc.—Fiction. 2. Dead—Fiction.
3. Sick—Fiction. 4. Conduct of life—Fiction.] I. Title.
PZ7.K6745Pie 2014
[Fic]—dc23
2013002235

The text of this book is set in 11.5-point Goudy.

Book design by Cathy Bobak

Printed in the United States of America

10 9 8 7 6 5 4 3 2 1

First Edition

To my first, and bestest, friend
Katie Taylor Ott

While we choreographed dances to "Thriller,"
watched Goonies and Annie,
won tickets at Chuck E. Cheese,
got Happy Meals and frozen custard,
dressed and re-dressed Cabbage Patch Kids, Care Bears,
and built forts in the back staircase of your house on Sylvia Street …

I knew about your open-heart surgeries, saw your scars,
but didn't understand the big picture until much later…

Katie, this story about kids who spend too much time in hospitals,
who fight for their futures, belongs to you…
My BFF of thirty years, you've earned your happiness,
And now we can dress and re-dress your beautiful baby girl…
To many more tomorrows. I love you.

CHAPTER ONE

I ignored the printed flyers for the upcoming homecoming; cheer-leaders encouraged school spirit with painted signs hanging haphazardly above rows of lockers. I spun the combo lock until open. I smashed against the metal lockers trying to stay out of everyone's way. Freshman jocks crowded below me, grabbing blindly while someone with hooves stepped on my foot but didn't notice.

The girl next to me smiled—what was her name? Becky? Becca? She told me once, back in freshman year when we were assigned these spots. I stared at the empty cavern of my locker and carefully removed the biology textbook and lab notebook I needed next period. She opened her locker door and a postcard fluttered out. I grabbed it, before it hit the floor and got trampled under clumsy jock feet. I studied the glossy photograph before handing it back. The image of an adobe chapel and cerulean skies was gorgeous. Haunting.

She waited and let me look, then answered my unspoken question. "That's El Santuario de Chimayo in New Mexico. Cool, huh? They say the dirt is miraculous."

I let go and she restuck it to the inside of her locker next to dozens of postcards seemingly from all over the world: Buddhas and temples, pyramids and caves, battlefields and shipwrecks. It was as if she'd crammed the Travel Channel into the tiny cubicle.

She saw my glance and said, "My cousin likes to send snail mail. We want to travel together someday."

"Oh." I didn't know what else to say, so I nodded. Had I gotten a postcard this year? Ever? Did I want to travel?

She shrugged as if waiting for harsh judgment and slammed her locker door before scurrying to her next class.

"Thanks," I called quietly, unsure why I felt the need to thank her and pleased she didn't seem to hear me.

I turned the corner toward bio and drew up sharply when the Skirt crew popped out of nowhere. I dodged and weaved, thinking I was in their way. *No. They're circling me.*

I stopped and froze, but didn't take my eyes off the Captain with her matching hair ribbons and school mascot in glittered tattoo on her cheek.

"You have a lot of hair." One of the Skirts spoke from behind me. I felt her hand on my braid, encircling it and tugging down the length until her hand was somewhere below my butt.

"Yeah." I clutched my books tighter against my chest, wishing instead for armor, or a Kevlar vest.

Another girl said, "We're holding a hair drive." It was as if she opened the floodgates because they all started talking at once, like a flock of gulls fighting over a clam.

"You know? For kids without hair."

"Wigs."

"You have a lot of hair."

"And it's so blond. Do you bleach it?"

I shrugged and shook my head, trying to answer and dodge their gazes at the same time. My hair was so purely blond it appeared white, especially in the summertime. I never dyed it, and I only trimmed the split ends every few months. I brushed it one hundred times before bed each night, even when I had the flu. I loved my hair. *I am my hair.*

The Skirts' Captain refocused the conversation. "West Haven is also holding a hair drive."

Like puppets, they reiterated, "There's a trophy."

"We want the trophy."

"We deserve the trophy."

As they saw the football team's quarterback approach, one Skirt tittered and called, "Hi, Leif, good luck in the game tonight!"

"Thanks, girls." He winked at the others and waved without stopping. But when his eyes met mine, he frowned and turned away. I wasn't worth a wink. Or a wave.

"We'll see him at the game. Focus," Captain snapped to the others.

"Uh." I tried to step around again. I was already late for class and the empty hallway made my heart thump and shift within my chest. What did they want? *My hair?*

"Look, we need your hair to win. You need an invitation to Kaylie's Halloween party."

"She does?" a Skirt asked from behind me.

"I do?" Seniors-only party. Only worthy underclassmen were exceptions. As a sophomore I didn't qualify, and I certainly wasn't worthy. "Oh."

I wanted to ask why, if they needed hair so badly, I saw none of their perfectly highlighted and toned lengths cut short for the cause. But I couldn't force the question out of my throat.

"So do we have a deal?" The Captain stepped closer. The circle tightened like a tourniquet. I felt hands reach for me.

How do I get out of here? Where's the roving teacher to break up loitering in the halls? "Uh. Let me think about it—"

She lunged closer. "What's there to think about? Don't you want to come to the party?"

"Can I bring a friend—" Part of me thought that might kill the deal. But part of me wanted to go to that party. At least be the one who was invited and said "No, thank you" on my terms. I wasn't brave enough to decline.

"Sure, whatever." She snapped gum and waved her hand toward the Skirts behind me.

"Okay, then I'll tell you tomorrow, first thing—" Trying to buy myself time and distance. Find oxygen not polluted with the latest cheap, and fruity, body spray. Formulate a plan. Like getting really sick before school tomorrow. Like appendicitis or tuberculosis. Mono wouldn't cut it with this crew. Janey-the-backflipper had it last year during Spirit Week and they put her bed on wheels and made her attend cheer finals.

"I have to ask—" But I didn't even finish my sentence before they whipped out the ponytail elastic and the gleaming shears. I froze. There, standing in hallway 6B, between classes, the hair I'd grown my entire life disappeared. I heard it, every snip, and snap, and slice. I knew hair didn't have nerve endings, but I felt each crack, each break of each strand.

In the three minutes between third and fourth period.

When I struggled, they grabbed and held with perfect manicures and manacle hands.

My breath faded, then returned.

My heart stuttered, then raced.

My eyes closed, then teared.

My hand groped until I felt the cold metal of a locker bank to my right. My head floated above my body. Faint white spots flew across my vision. I leaned against that piece of wall as if it was the only thing keeping me upright.

"Are you okay?" One of them peered down at me as though I was an odd science experiment. I wondered if she'd catch me if I fainted, or just move to the side and let me splat against the cement floor.

I didn't speak, didn't answer her stupid question as the late bell rang.

"This totally puts us over the top. Trophy time." They high-fived and turned to leave.

I managed to say, "Please?" Was I begging for my hair back? Was I begging to time travel? I knew I wasn't asking for the party invitation, and yet that was what they heard.

One Skirt thrust the flyer into my hand. An ugly sneer shiny with lip gloss instructed me, "Don't dress like a prude, though, okay?"

With that, they disappeared, spiriting away my braided hair, into the maze of hallways. Hair I brushed one hundred times a night before bed and shampooed with organic natural ingredients. Hair I let fall in front of my face so I didn't have to make eye contact with the classmates on either side of me.

I reached a hand up to my head, palming neck skin and

airspace I hadn't recently noticed. If ever. The back of my neck felt soft and downy, like brand-new. Like it hadn't been in the sun or wind or rain. Ever. The ridges on either side of my neck, the concavity between them, felt especially tingly, like the nerves there fired rapidly, trying to figure out what happened.

Hair fell against my chin in odd points, but the whole back of my head was a chopped-up mess of layers. I headed for the bathroom. I didn't know if I wanted to see the damage.

So fast. That happened so fast.

The bathroom door swung shut behind me, and I felt a storm of desolation threaten to cut off my air supply. *Can't breathe. Can't breathe.*

I leaned over the sink, unable to focus my eyes on the mirror's reflection. Choking. My heart raced. My stomach clenched painfully, leaden, and burned.

Sounds of crying filled the bathroom with sniffles and snorts and sobs and . . . for a moment, I thought I'd lost my tenuous grip on my sanity. *No, it's not me.*

I turned toward the stalls and my bag thumped against the paper towel dispenser. The sounds cut off as if the crier held her breath, knowing she wasn't alone. I opened my mouth. *What do I say? "Wanna cry together?"*

Instead, I ran from the bathroom and from the sadness that seemed to cling to me like a bad reputation.

I *wasn't* watching where I was going, because next thing I knew I was sprawled on the ground and Vivian-the-monster-cough-girl bounced up, trying to pull me to my feet. Then she coughed like she was giving birth to an alien. Ew. She wiped her mouth with her hand.

"I'm sorry. I'm always too much in a hurry. Can't sit still when I don't have to. Are you okay? I didn't hurt you, did I?" She gave the door a scathing look, as if it had gotten her in trouble on purpose.

I didn't answer, just nodded.

"You sure you're okay? I gotta get to chem lab—I'm so behind and there's a test today—but I can walk you to the office if you want to see a nurse? Are you sick?" She whitened, then backed away a little, as if the thought of illness scared her. *I must look really terrible for her to give me that horrified expression.*

Shaking my head, I simply turned away and walked out of school. Mrs. Harding, the school's ancient secretary, who had an amazing memory and name recall, shouted, "Stop! Jessica Chai, you do not have permission to leave school early today."

My step hitched and for a moment I wondered about breaking the rules. I didn't break the rules. *Ever.* But then, behind me, someone did me the favor of puking, hacking all over the reception desk, and diverted all attention from the front doors. From me. Maybe it was Vivian. Or the crier. I didn't look back. I didn't care. I needed out. *Now.*

I acted like a class-cutting pro. *Screw it.* I hiked toward the Metro bus stop. *I will get myself home. Get home and fix it. Borrow a hat from my brother. A scarf from my mother.*

If I'd had any idea what losing my hair meant, I wouldn't have gone to school at all that day.

CHAPTER TWO

"**Jessica?** Oh my good lord, what did you do?" The usual polite veneer flaked off my mother's voice because my appearance shocked her.

What's she doing home early?

I didn't have to turn around to imagine my mother's eyes bulging out of her head. The whites rolled back like a horse scenting smoke. I swallowed. *She'll make this about her in . . . one . . . two . . .*

"And I couldn't go with you to the salon? To see my girl become a beautiful swan? Who did you see? This isn't even a five-dollar discount cut." She peered at me like I was a circus sideshow. Her perfectly manicured nails bit into my upper arms as she twisted and jerked me around.

"It happened at school. For little-girl wigs." I'd been lying so long to my parents, before and after the divorce, about my life, that it never occurred to me to tell her the truth.

"Oh dear. Don't they know who you are? How did this happen? I kept my hair long until my senior year." She touched my head, my shoulders, as if trying to feel out understanding, rather than listening.

I know.

I shivered, unused to her touch. Unused to her interaction.

"This is a mess." She caught herself and backed up a step. Back into her own personal space. From there, she didn't touch me but ran her hands around the outside of my space bubble. The more she studied me, the more disappointed she seemed. "Did they pay beauty school students to do this, or the special education department? Atrocious."

"Mother." I blinked at the venom spewed in that single word. *Atrocious? The hack job or me?* I wasn't sure.

"Well, I'm sorry, but you did a nice thing and you should be prettier for it, not looking like a pile of . . ."

Insert excrement and wrinkled nose.

She brightened almost instantly. "I know. I will call Dmitry right now. He'll fit us in tomorrow morning and we'll get you red-carpet ready and go to lunch and shopping afterward for a fresh wardrobe."

"Tomorrow is a school day," I reminded her, trying not to dampen her enthusiasm too fast. So little about me made her happy.

"You can't go to school looking like this." She shook her head and vetoed scarves and hats and hoods. "I'll call in favors. We'll go now instead. Right now."

"But—"

"We'll buy a new dress too. Wouldn't you like that? You'll take a mental-health day tomorrow. Then you can go to the gallery fund-raiser with me Saturday night. It'll be fun."

Her latest paramour must be busy.

She didn't wait for me to say yea or nay. Simply dialed her cell and demanded to speak with Dmitry. Listening to her explain what happened to me, she made it sound like I was both a saint and a victim of a terrible crime. She didn't know how close she came to the victim part.

"We're set up for three o'clock. Shall I make dinner reservations at Allehambra's? Everyone's talking about their tapas, and the chef is supposed to be Michelin-star-worthy."

I didn't have time to respond, not like it would have mattered, before she dialed again. Then she whisked me toward the door with a "We have to hurry."

I had no idea who to expect. I'd never met Dmitry. Never been invited to my mother's sanctum of beauty and potions.

The floating notes of flutes and smooth piano played throughout the salon via live musicians stationed in the lobby. Marble, chrome, and glass made the salon seem both modern and like Ann Boleyn might have had her hair done here. Right before they beheaded her, of course.

I have also never, ever, heard a man cluck and fuss quite like this.

"Isn't it awful?" my mother commented under her breath, but loud enough to draw sympathetic glances from middle-aged women around us who wore diamonds to get their hair done. They shared her pain.

Dmitry didn't talk to me. He spoke directly to my mother . . . when he talked . . . but mostly he simply made sounds of a panicked crow trapped in a plastic bag. All hands and fingers, he tugged and yanked, lifted and stared at my hair. At my face. He called over other black-clad shiny airbrushed professionals, holding my hair just so while they fussed and babbled and studied each strand with emphatic nods and clacking combs. Finally, like a sports team, they broke apart and Dmitry turned me to face the softly lit mirror.

"You have Emma Watson cheekbones and Halle Berry lips," he declared before huddling with my mother six feet away.

"Thanks?" I said, unable to even glance at my reflection.

"I'll be in the spa. Dmitry will make you beautiful." Mother disappeared behind frosted doors, and that was when the work began in earnest. Smiles were replaced by concentrated scowls; someone covered the mirror at Dmitry's station. *Do I look bad enough to break glass?*

I felt as if I was being readied to be sacrificed to the great hair god volcano.

There was a girl who washed, another girl who dried, one who rewet; there were several different applications of sweet-smelling glop, a rinse, another dry, until I closed my eyes and stopped counting. Then Dmitry hovered over me with flashing blades and lightning reflexes. I was afraid to move and thereby risk mortal wounds. We didn't speak. He only stopped to repeat things I thought had already happened. Like everything else, my knowledge of hair care was insignificant and wrong.

He snapped. Literally snapped his fingers, and a team of hovering sprites, also head to toe in black and clicking in towering heels, bustled around my face. Applying brushes dabbed in potions and lotions and other applications of color to my face. I held my body immobile like a rabbit fixed in the gaze of a coyote. I watched with an odd detachment but never caught a random glimpse of my reflection.

Then, after three hours and twelve minutes, six different goop applications, pieces of foil and something that looked like it came off a spaceship, three shampoos, and four different products applied during the blow-drying process, Dmitry appeared satisfied.

My mother gawked at me with tears in her eyes.

I didn't know if they were happy tears or horrified ones, because her face remained smoothly youthful and devoid of expression.

"Oh, my baby. She's finally—"

"Supreme," Dmitry declared. "Now close eyes and I spin you." He made eye contact with me for the first time.

I squeezed them, bracing myself against the expectation that seemed to suck the oxygen out of the room. All activity ceased; even the musicians seemed to hold their notes.

As Dmitry turned the chair around he commanded, "Open your eyes."

The first thing I saw in the mirror was Mother standing behind me, her hands clasped in prayer-like fervor.

Then I focused on the woman reflected back at me.

Woman? Me?

My naturally white-blond hair seemed to be spun of gold and sunlight and moonlight. A fairy pixie with huge eyes framed by long full lashes stared back at me. Brows of melted gold arched in question, and in statement, above them. My skin glowed as if polished and dusted with light. My hair was so short, it served as more of a cap of fringe around my face. Facets of diamonds seemed to float and caress the air around my head. Twin curls caressed my cheeks and cradled my ears. My lips were shiny and pink, as if I'd gorged on the freshest berries. Even my hated upturned nose seemed itself a cute addition to an otherwise orchestrated collection of perfected features.

"That's me?" I asked, my voice breathy and unsure.

The salon broke into amazed applause, subdued and polite,

but I saw the expressions on the faces of the stylists—not at my surprise beauty, but at Dmitry's astonishing skill in finding it. As if they'd decided there was nothing that could be done for me when I'd first walked in.

My mother had never seemed so proud to claim me. She walked with her arm around me to Allehambra's and treated the crowds to a deferent tolerance, as if she were the Queen of England.

From our corner table, Mother scanned the restaurant as if waiting for someone more important, or at least more interesting, than me. I saw the flash of panic when she realized she hadn't spent this kind of time with me since I was a baby. Why had I let her reel me in this time?

Silence stretched until even the waiter filling our water glasses looked like he wanted to present a conversation topic to break the ice. I nibbled on a cracker. Turned out we weren't eating tapas at a tapas restaurant. *How many Michelin stars does a salad rate?*

"So, Jessica, have you thought about your college major? As a legacy, you have options."

I think it was always assumed I'd go to college, but the closer I got, the more I felt as if my parents were sizing me up to see if I was worth the quarter-of-a-million-dollar investment that their private alma matter required. *Assuming I get in.*

I nodded. "Um, sure. I took the PSAT last week."

"I thought you had to be a junior to take that?" Some people's foreheads creased with questions, but not my mother's.

"They have sophomores take it too—they say it helps the school with scheduling." Basically, they used it to weed out

13

the vocational kids and the borderline mediocre ones from the smart and genius ones. My high school had close to two thousand students—most of us tracked classes based on how smart we appeared on tests. It was acceptable segregation.

"Oh, well, how did you do?" She sipped her water as if to make it last.

"It went okay." *Say something else, tell her more, make up something if you have to.*

The waiter set down the half-size house salads in front of us. Hers without dressing and mine with a barely there vinaigrette. I saw Mother's half sneer as I dripped the dressing over the lettuce. The plate was barely larger than a teacup saucer, and there were maybe six bites of produce, total. We never lingered over dessert, not even birthday cakes, and heaven forbid we have a substantial lunch. My mother wasn't fat, but by all memory I'd never seen her indulge in anything fatty, or hearty, for that matter. It was as if she was so tightly controlled that any given bite might mean the whole of her soul unraveling.

A dozen deep breaths later, she offered a new topic. "I have my book club meeting Monday night." She spoke while cutting a lettuce leaf into sixteen tiny pieces. One so small it barely stayed on a single fork tine long enough to make it into her mouth.

Grab and hold on. "Oh? What's the book?"

She blotted her lips with the napkin and finished chewing. I almost counted along with her. Sixteen chews, then swallow. She'd tried to instill this magical number in me from toddler time on. "Some novel about friends and divorces. It got wonderful reviews on Amazon."

"You didn't read it?" I knew she hadn't. She didn't read. She went to book club for the gossip and the wine. She left the read-ing to online reviewers. I highly doubted anyone in her club actually read the book itself. *Ever.*

"No time. You know how busy I am."

I nodded, trying to keep my mouth full. I didn't want to hear about weight creeping in when I wasn't watching. *Ninja calories.*

Mother shooed away the dessert tray and set her credit card on the table without even checking the bill. "Shall we go find a lovely outfit for us?" She seemed relieved to move again.

We hadn't been inside the city's oldest, and most notable, department store ten minutes before she tried to make me into her, one piece of clothing at a time.

"This would look lovely on you." Mother held up a pair of slacks and a beige blouse that had the personality of a uniform and the ability to insult no one. Of course, they cost more than most car payments, and we were two floors from any department my peers might frequent. Was money the reason my parents split? All Father talked about was saving, and Mother seemed to shop as her hobby.

"Hmm." I was noncommittal. *What do I say? She's trying. Right?*

"Something else, then?" She set them back and shooed away a salesperson. She oohed and aahed over a tweed pantsuit and a silk blouse that looked like variations on the theme of her closet. We worked our way around the floor until we were within eye-sight of the special-occasion section. Sequins and ruffles, shiny jewels sparkled against midnight draping on mannequins with ballerina proportions. Something eager must have shown on my face, because Mother picked up on my expression and nudged me closer to the gowns. *Maybe she hopes we can bond over sparkles?*

"I need a suitable dress for the Art Museum Gala. I have one I can wear, but I'd rather get a new piece of fabulous." Mother shared this as if I knew about all of her social events, as if I was invited to any.

"The black and white gala?" I winced, hoping it wasn't the masquerade- or the ocean-themed.

"Something black, I think." She nodded.

I tried to appear interested but felt a pull away from the artfully displayed but interchangeable little black dresses and toward a creation the color of clear sunlit sky. I'd never seen anything like it. Layers of every shade of blue blended together and floated like clouds; just a hint of glimmer, like the first stars in the evening sky, hinted that there was something spectacular to come around the bend.

"Oh my." Mother stopped behind me. Her sigh danced the hairs on the back of my neck and sent a shiver down my spine.

I waited for her to make a comment about it being garish, or too much, or pointing out that I didn't have any gala to wear it to. *There's only one and it's my size.*

"You should try that on," she said.

Really?

The salesperson hovering nearby studied me head to toe and grabbed the padded hanger, whisking it toward the fitting lounge. How did she know my size by glancing? That's talent. *How do you figure out that's your talent?*

I felt my breath leave my body and my heart thump. Was it possible to fall in love with a dress? "I don't—" I felt Mother's enthusiasm deflate as if I was purposefully being difficult. "Sure."

Mother beamed and asked the sales associate to help her find a suitable black dress.

A dressing room large enough to accommodate the football team, and a fainting couch, filled with the gaggle of women. According to them, it was the flecks of Swarovski crystals that made the layers of tulle and chiffon dance. I felt like a shooting star in the magic of space. The material was hand-dyed and hand-stitched.

There were the right undergarments and height of slipper heels to haggle over—Mother and the team of three sales associates discussed and lobbied and thrust opinions at me. They could have been trading stock futures, or baseball statistics, for all I understood or cared. My heart melted, and I couldn't stop smiling at myself in the mirror. I was elfin, fairy princess–esque, utterly and completely not myself. I had the slightest of curves in the right places, and my pale skin almost seemed to glow against the fabric.

I didn't want to take the dress off, but the attention slowly turned from me to her, as it was bound to do. The retail team worked hard, running and suggesting, making sure we headed toward the counter with every possible piece. The saleswomen blended seemingly back in the racks and nooks around them, as if by magic.

Mother saw friends and air-kissed over small talk. They suggested quick coffee. I had no desire to sit and try not to look bored out of my mind.

"I must talk to Cynthia," Mother told me under her breath, and walked me toward the checkout counter.

Quick! Come up with a getaway plan. "I've been invited to a Halloween party." My dress floated as if it were alive. I couldn't wait to wrap myself in it again and be the girl who wore it. She was interesting and beautiful and noticeable.

The briefest of shocks flickered in Mother's eyes before she smoothly replied, "Of course you have. I should have asked what your plans were for tomorrow night. Well then, I'll speak with my friends and these lovely associates will find you something more appropriate for a Halloween party." Again the flock flapped forward as if on cue.

Brilliant. As much as I hated the idea of having help from strangers while I shopped, it was better than trying to make small talk about people I didn't know, or care about, with my mother's frenemies. I saw their expressions—they were vultures clothed in couture. No way were they real friends. Not that I knew what real friends looked, or sounded, like. I didn't have any of my own to compare. *Call it a gut feeling.*

"We don't have to get the dress," I offered, my heart pangs ignored.

"Nonsense, I'm sure there will be an upcoming occasion that will be perfection for."

I smiled and kissed her on the cheek. She couldn't cover the surprise and handed me her card. "I'll see you in about an hour? Take care of those beautiful gowns for us, please," she instructed.

I nodded, we all nodded, as Mother squared her shoulders and headed toward the café and her friends. Part of me wondered why she needed to talk to Cynthia and part of me focused on trying to ditch the commissioned help. "I don't need help—I'm heading down to the juniors' floor," I said, and they looked relieved to not leave their department.

I touched the hem of the wishing-star dress as it disappeared into the fabric bag. I couldn't wait to wear it again.

If Mother had known she was buying the dress she'd bury me

in, I wonder if she'd have chosen something different, or if she'd have still gone to java talk with those biddies.

SAMUEL

Samuel pulled a postcard from his stack, barely glancing at the photograph of adobe caves. His mother was at it again. He smacked the stamp down and picked up his pen to jot the next address and a quick note. Four hours of dialysis a day required inventive ways to pass the time: snail mail to relatives and friends, The-Daily-Miracle.com, and inventing video games.

"You're not listening to me." Ma slapped her hand over his. The pressure forced the pen to drag a black line down the side of the card.

Sam sighed. She didn't understand. He couldn't make her see it his way, but he wished she'd give it a rest. "I will not pray for a transplant," he repeated. *Again.*

"Samuel—you must. We've tried everything else. You must pray."

Pray for someone to die? How can she be serious?

"I will pray for a miracle. Miracles are okay." Miracles didn't necessarily mean tragedy for another family. Death was a thin blade—who it cut and when was unknown. Why didn't she understand that?

"You and your miracles." She paced to the window.

He knew she thought his website, The-Daily-Miracle.com, a silly waste of his energy. His snail mail even sillier. She wanted him to go conquer and piss on trees and be a man outside among the bears and warriors. Not inside with screens and nerds. Her desperation for him to live at all morphed into something else entirely. They'd had this fight so many times he didn't need to see the script to know his lines. "A transplant means someone else died."

"And that's not a miracle? You know, with your PRA count—" She broke off, stifling a sob before suppressing it and turning with fire in her eyes. "You believe Christ died for you and that you're worthy of that. Why not someone else?"

"It's not that simple, Ma." Sam turned back to his computer. "Christ died for everyone. All of us. Not just me. As did Juan Martinez of Balbao, a supposed and little-known reincarnation of the Messiah from the twentieth century. Buddha lived for the world's enlightenment. How's that? Muhammad was a prophet bearing Allah's words. Christ was not alone."

She leaned over his back and squeezed his shoulders. "Don't start quoting your hobby to me. Yes, yes, it is that simple."

Sam shook his head. "Christ died for all of humanity, for all time."

"Who says you're not going to impact the entire world? You are not going to die, Samuel. I forbid it." She stomped out and slammed the door. There was no arguing with her when she was in one of these moods.

He logged on to MiracleMakers; his online gaming community understood him. Twenty-one thousand, three hundred, and forty-seven people currently playing to save the world understood his dilemma. He prayed for a miracle, but he wouldn't pray for someone to die to save him. How could he be more worthy of a long life than someone else?

VIVIAN

There was a ten-ton moon-rock (Pantone 17-1210) elephant sitting on Vivian's chest. There had to be. It was the only plausible explanation. The elephant began dancing. Swing dancing in bottle-green (Pantone 17-5722) Chuck Taylors. And giggling.

Vivian forced the elephant to sit next to her and be quiet so she could listen to the doctor talk to her parents. She hated when they talked about her as if she wasn't in the room. Dr. Feilstone didn't usually; he knew better after all these years. She must be really sick. The kind of sick that buried her friends.

Dr. Feilstone continued. "She's been very healthy and shown she can manage her disease well up until this point. There's nothing she could have done to prevent this attack. So I see no reason why they won't move her up the donor list for lungs and, now, a heart."

A transplant? She didn't need new lungs; she needed the zookeepers to come take the elephant home and she'd be okay. Her heart was fine. She had a painting to finish. It was important. If only she could remember who she'd been painting. She tried to speak, but they weren't listening and couldn't have understood her over the machine crammed into her throat and mouth. Adding machines to aid her breathing and body functions meant it was bad. *Say good-bye kind of bad.*

Dr. Feilstone frowned. "I have to caution you. Even if a set of donor lungs and a heart become available, it won't stop the CF issues she has elsewhere. It will merely make it possible for her to live right now."

Donor lungs? A heart? How did someone donate vital organs and keep liv—? They didn't. They couldn't. These meds made

Vivian loopy and slow. Of course she knew transplants happened all the time. But those were vague conversations about down the road. When she was older and the CF took its exacting toll on her body. When they were all out of options and all other treatments failed.

"We're lucky to have a top transplant team here at the medical center. This will make it easier on Vivian to get the best care. I've asked Dr. Alexander to join us to answer any questions you might have. He's head of the transplant team. And we've called her primary CF specialist to consult as well."

The door opened and Vivian turned her head toward the bright light.

She recognized her dad's voice. "What if we don't find a donor?"

A new voice answered in clipped business tones the color of suitable dark blue (Pantone 19-3921). "She will not make it out of the hospital this weekend. It's simply not reversible with current methods of treatment. She hasn't responded to anything. She needs lungs. A heart. Now." Was that Dr. Alexander matter-of-factly declaring her life over?

Vivian's mom made sounds of heartbreak. Vivian wanted to reach out and reassure her. It would be okay. It would all be okay. They'd known her whole life that she would not live forever. Thirty-five was probably the outside edge of possible. She'd made it past year six, then eleven, then fourteen. Day by day, she'd made it this far. Maybe this was as far as her journey went.

She imagined her dad locking his jaw and crossing his arms, steeling himself to ask the question she knew came next. Sure enough, he rumbled, "What are the odds? What are the numbers that it's even possible for her to be high enough on the list and for someone to . . ." His words trailed off but they all knew what he was asking.

Vivian tried to lift her hand to get their attention, but they weren't looking at her. She watched Dr. Alexander's shadow, saw him pause.

The doctor spoke with slow deliberation, as if carefully weighing each word as deed. "It's Halloween weekend, with a high probability of Saturday-night parties. The Weather Channel forecasts one of the Pacific Northwest's famous powerful November storms rolling in a bit early—which means lots of rain and wind. These are all factors in favor of donor organs becoming available. I've been doing this for thirty years. Someone's going to die tonight. That's all I can tell you for sure."

CHAPTER THREE

The wind's fingers snaked through my hair and sent chills down my spine as it flicked the bare spots behind my ears. I kept the windows down to chase out the perfume Mother had insisted on spritzing all over me. I smelled like a middle-aged woman heading to a garden party. *Eww.*

Even with my bag on it, the party flyer threatened to take off as a gust picked it up and danced it out of reach across the passenger seat. I hit the window buttons and the glass glided closed. I needed that flyer for directions. *Where the heck am I? Where is this party?*

New, crisp skinny jeans with artful and expensive rips complemented tall black leather boots, a lace camisole, and a bolero jacket with a skull woven into the lace along my back. A mask of molded lace lay across my eyes and nose, tied with delicate velvet ribbons at the back of my head. It made my eyes seem twice their size and an interesting magical shade of gray instead of the usual boring blah. I didn't take off the mask for fear that I'd lose my nerve completely. My hair was both spiked and tousled like it hadn't taken hours to get it exactly so. Dmitry and his elves made it seem so easy.

I smiled into the rearview mirror. For once I looked danger-ous. Like a rock 'n' roll pixie with a mischievous secret. I stifled a giggle that bordered on hysterical.

What secret?

Tonight, I am someone else.

Tonight, I can have all the secrets I want.

Maybe changing my life started with my hair. Halloween. Wasn't that what the holiday was about? Transforming into some-one else? Being whoever you wanted to be instead of yourself?

I would finally be the pretty, popular girl who everyone noticed. Not just an improved me, but a whole new girl. I was the girl who wielded the scissors, who didn't care if it was okay to hack off someone's limb. This girl smiled and fluttered her eyes at boys, who grinned back.

That's who I am tonight. Maybe forever. Who knew? Anything seemed possible.

I turned up the satellite radio, listening as Ingrid Michaelson's voice soared. *"I'm a ghost. . . ."*

Tonight, I wasn't a ghost. I wasn't invisible. I wasn't nothing or no one.

Heading around a curve, oncoming headlights blinded me. I gripped the steering wheel. *Where is this house?* Out in the weeds, far from the city limits, far from well-marked streets and stop-lights. Far from anything I knew. *New.*

I reached down and grabbed the flyer. The party supposedly started after the football game. Though rumor had it the party started well before and simply took a game break before rev-ving back up again. I wasn't arriving until after ten. I refused to acknowledge that usually on Saturday nights I was in bed watch-ing whatever behind-the-scenes celebrity crime was profiled.

I slowed to read the cut-and-paste directions again. *Did I miss a turn? No, keep going.*

The tree-lined two-lane road felt like a squeezing tunnel, as if I were driving into an otherworldly reality. I shivered. My headlights picked up the shine of metal and I saw empty beer cans littering the road. *Must be getting closer.*

Movement to the side of the road forced me to slam the brakes hard.

A deer. Four-point buck. Sneaking a peek out from the bushes.

I eased back into drive. Behind me, an SUV roared up, seemingly from out of nowhere, honking. I sped up, wishing there was a place to pull over so I could follow them instead. They sure seemed like they knew where they were going. I was in their way.

Where's the switchback?

The road abruptly turned and I recognized one of the instructions. "Take the next right after the switchback." *The next right? That's a ravine. Isn't it?* I peered at the landscape as the SUV laid on its horn and swerved around me toward oncoming traffic.

I heard shouts and insults but only made out a few words. Nothing original.

Someone threw a bottle out the back of the truck toward my windshield. I ducked, instinctively, my foot off the gas pedal but frozen above the brake. No way to move. I saw the future, and the present, as it happened in slow motion around me.

The sound of breaking glass and the crunch of impact made me strangle the wheel. Lights blinded me as clear liquid spread over the cracks and obscured my view. I heard horns and screams. Frantic to escape, I spun the wheel and hit the brakes. Light refracted into the cracks of the windshield.

Pretty.

Am I there yet?

If I remembered hitting my head, or getting knocked out, I might have known how much time passed before I came to.

I wasn't sure how long I'd been unconscious, but someone must have helped me out of the car. *Where is the car?*

I glanced around. Faces were blurry and unrecognizable. I still reeked of Mother's perfume but also of something else. Warm urine? *Did I pee myself? Please don't let anyone notice.*

I tried to fit tighter into myself, hugging my arms, crossing my legs.

Shouts and flurries of movement, people carrying bags marched with purpose and intention all around me. Almost as if they didn't see me, or know I was in the accident.

The smell of hard booze clung to me and the world had a strange phosphoric red glow from flares cops set up along the road. A crowd of people I recognized vaguely from school huddled near one barrier and whispered to one another. They cried and seemed much more sober than when they sped by me and tossed that bottle back.

Where is my car? Mother will ground me for life if I wrecked it.

A hush fell over the onlookers as arms wrapped around a full stretcher appeared from over the edge of the ravine.

Wait, who's wearing my costume? Who is she and what's she doing over in the trees?

As soon as they were on level ground, someone straddled the girl's chest and started CPR, while another man attached one of those blue inflatable balloons to her mouth. She must have been in an accident too.

They came toward me and I tried to move out of their way but no one seemed to notice me. *So much for starting a new life tonight.*

A policewoman walked toward the group of spectators and I heard her ask, "Anyone know this girl's name? Recognize her? Are you friends with her?"

A second policeman held a copy of the same party flyer as if it were contaminated, and started speaking into his radio. *I'm glad I'm not at the party; they're about to be raided by the police.*

"She goes to our school."

The cop turned sharply. "Was she going to this party?"

"Uh—"

She shook her head. "I don't care about you kids, we need to find her family."

A boy I didn't recognize spoke up. "Sure, it's a big deal every year."

"She has to be friends with the group to get invited. So someone knows her."

"I don't know her name." Several more teens shrugged and shook their heads. The sentiment was all the same. They didn't know the girl.

As the cop walked the periphery, I heard them each in turn express regret, or shrug, or guess, in terrible ways, about the girl's identity. *She's like me. She's an invisible.*

"Is she going to be okay?" One cheerleader pushed toward the front of the pack.

"She's going to the hospital. Doctors will assess her there."

"Is she, like, dead?" her boyfriend asked.

The policewoman paused. "I'm not a doctor," she answered before she walked away to confer with other first responders.

Poor girl, no one knew her. *Maybe I know her? Why aren't they asking me?* I walked toward the ambulance, intent on seeing her, when they slammed the doors in my face and it started moving.

Rude.

"Tow truck's here!" one fireman called out as he passed me to herd the crowd out of the way.

"It's gonna be tricky to get that Prius unwrapped at that angle."

"Yeah, dumb kid, probably was texting and not paying attention."

"They find the phone?" the policewoman asked.

"Nah, but they brought up the registration for your ID." He handed her the packet. *That folio looks like Mother's. And her handwriting.*

They moved the barricades for the ambulance to leave and the truck to enter. Just as I was leaning over the registration packet to see who the owner of the car was, it felt as if I was jerked off my feet backward.

"Help!" I screamed, but no one moved.

LEIF

While the scoreboard glowed 31–28, somewhere in the stands scouts from USC, Texas, and University of Florida waited to see if Leif held his own against the opposing senior quarterback. Go Sea Lions.

Leif listened to his dad call out commands from the stands. He knew his phone was blowing up with texts from his dad telling him what to do differently, better, more like a winner. His dad didn't, or couldn't, comprehend that unlike his teammates, Leif left his phone in the locker room. No distractions. He especially didn't possess his dad's win-at-all-costs mentality.

The ref blew the fourth quarter start whistle and Leif's heart thumped a little harder. The kicked football hung in the air and his defense charged. The opposing team's kick-return specialist annihilated the line, finding holes to run semitrucks through. Get him! Get him!

Leif closed his eyes as the runner crossed into the end zone with the ball cradled snugly in his arm. Jesus. The guys all but stepped out of his way. Dammit, this is a big-enough game without giving them points.

What were the scouts thinking? Did they want to see him succeed or fail? Who was on his side? He forced himself not to study the crowd while his team's kick-return unit took the field. They got six yards before being stuffed at the twenty. That was a perfect kick; Leif had to run lots of clock and scramble for inches. *It's now or never.*

He heard his dad's voice in his head and felt the hand heavy on his shoulder. "Show them what a Leolin is made of. Nothing but number one. Son, make me proud."

Leif crammed his black mouth guard in place and snapped on his helmet as he stormed the field.

Three downs and he struggled to make a positive play happen. It was as if his offensive line was already in the locker room partying this Halloween night. Their heads were anywhere but on the field. Dammit.

"Focus!" he shouted in the huddle over the crowd noise. "We need a touchdown."

He'd do it on his own if he had to.

The whistle blew. The ball hiked.

In slow motion, he saw the hole open up and he lifted his arm to pump the throw. The line shifted.

Wrong way.

Cover me!

Leif didn't so much see the defender coming as hear him. Heard his breath, felt the hot, stale air push through the face mask. Leif let the ball go as the defender lowered his helmet in a bizarre contortion and aimed up with his cleats.

What is happening?

The pop and snap registered first and sounded like special effects in a movie.

A giant question mark hung in the lights above the field as Leif stared up at the cloudless, star-filled sky. *Can anyone else see that?*

Silence filled the stadium. The stars held their breath.

"He's in shock. We've got to stop this bleeding."

Leif tried to move. Who was bleeding?

"Hey, man, stay down. You can't get up." Leif's center held his shoulders down.

Cold seeped up through Leif's uniform and pads. He opened his mouth, trying to speak, trying to breathe. Trying to think.

Sirens screamed, the only sound for miles around. *Where'd everybody go?*

Flashing lights moved in from Leif's peripheral vision, closer, until everyone huddled over him seemed to be strobing in red and blue.

"Give us room, guys. Back it up!"

They can't drive on the field. What are they doing?

Did I drink too much at the party?

As if someone hit a switch, the lights and noise rushed back in until Leif couldn't keep his stomach quiet and turned his head to vomit in the grass.

Great, pansy-ass move to puke in front of the scouts.

The world swirled and blackened.

Leif fought to open his eyes, to listen to the conversation, the raised voices, the argument in the distance. He touched soft fabric under his hands, not turf. His eyelids felt glued shut but he struggled to open them enough to see, to understand.

Is the game over already? Who's talking?

He blinked crusty bits out of his sight and realized he was still on his back, but instead of seeing stars above him there was a pocked ceiling of industrial tiles. His head seemed heavier than normal and his neck behaved like a limp noodle. Carefully, he cataloged and tried to make sense. White sheets draped his body and IV tubes were taped to his hands. A pinching binder clip was attached to his index finger. A green-striped curtain surrounded his bed like a wraparound shower curtain. Shower? Bed? Where was he?

The voices outside the curtain strengthened. Angry? Determined?

Leif strained to understand. He was operating underwater. *Is this what being drunk feels like?* He never drank. His body was his temple.

Machines beeped and footsteps pounded, but he recognized his dad's voice. Leif propped himself up on his elbows. There, against the curtain, his mother's shadow talked with her hands, like a freak puppet show. He picked out words and tried to move farther upright to a seated position instead of lying flat. Pain stung with far-reaching tentacles but also perked up his brain. The hospital? He was in the hospital? His thoughts sharpened, swimming to the surface of the medication.

"Don't yell. We don't want to wake Leif," Dad commanded, grabbing Mom's shoulders in consolation or restraint. Or both.

They thought he was asleep behind the curtain? He needed to listen. The truth was on the other side of that curtain.

Leif fought the medication because he knew his parents were never honest with him. Win at all costs. They'd kept his grandmother's death a secret while he was at football camp last summer.

"He is fine. He'll be fine," his mother screeched. "Just give him ice and a few days of ibuprofen and he'll be back in full form by league playoffs."

Leif didn't think they put people in rooms like this if ice and Advil were enough. Waves of sleepiness crashed over him and he struggled not to drown. *Listen! Focus!*

A voice he didn't know said, "He will not play again this season, Mrs. Leolin. Your son is very badly hurt. He'll probably need additional surgeries in the future. At this point, we will do all we can to reconstruct his joints using donor tissues, once we are certain his head injury is stable."

Not play? There was a mistake. They must be talking about someone else. He just took a hard hit. That happened all the time. He needed to get out of bed, move the curtain, and show them.

Leif shoved his legs toward the side of the bed and was immediately hit by a wall of nausea. Dark spots danced behind his tightly squished eyelids, and cold sweat bathed a tremble across his body. He sagged against the pillows until the pain eased. He didn't try to move, only to listen.

"Titanium? What are you using?" Mom jabbed with her questions and half swallowed a sob.

"Natural materials will give him the best shot at recovery. But there will be man-made components as well. It all depends on how it looks when we get in there. I'm sorry I can't be more specific until we have eyes on the damage."

"But he'll be able to play in the off-season." Dad didn't ask questions, only made statements.

"Sir, with all due respect, I will be happy if your son can walk again normally."

They couldn't be talking about him. Were they?

Giving in, not wanting to think, Leif sank deep into the blank waves.

MISTY

Stabbing pain ripped Misty's gut as if an ice pick impaled her side. She curled deeper into herself, praying for it to stop. Death seemed to want her and she wanted the pain to stop. She willed herself to stop breathing, to give in, and take the Reaper's hand. Soaked with sweat, she didn't have the ability to toss back the blankets. Raging with a furnace inside, the last drips of moisture mingled with her tears. She lay on a pallet of stained mattress and discarded rugs, in the sleeping corner of the tiny apartment, listening as curses and swears were hurtled like bullets and bayonets. Her parents fought. Again. She'd begged the school's nurse not to call home. The nurse didn't listen.

"I had to leave work. They called and said she was sick. I got there as fast as I could. I told them we'd take her to the doctor." Her mom's accent thickened and English threatened to retreat in the face of overreaching anger and years of frustration.

Misty visualized her papa's expression. If she had bet on his next words, she'd have won.

"How do we pay for that?" he yelled.

Her mother must have shrugged. As if Misty was sick on purpose. "She's our daughter."

"You think I don't know that?" He threw something made of fragile glass, shattering it against the wall. Her mother shrieked about cleaning it up. They deteriorated into jumbled threats and promises.

Misty's eyes leaked tears and she swallowed down the urge to vomit again. Fear that she'd puke up all her insides if she started, ravaged the last of her control. She kept trying to hold her breath against the pain. Breathing hurt. She felt every heartbeat down in her gut.

There were more sounds of glass breaking and pans being thrown. Her parents reverted to their native tongue and she tried to pick out words. Money. Doctors. Sacrifice. Job.

Listening to her parents fight over money, over her, shredded her heart. She should be working instead of going to school, but her parents agreed she would graduate from college. Make enough to support them and the family still back in the old country. Pain crashed into her, curling her toes and cramping her calves. This blurred all the edges of thought.

Her youngest brother, George, slithered over to her and

whispered, "Don't worry, I called 911. The ambulance is coming." He let her strangle his fingers.

Misty tried to stop him, but all she could manage was a tight hold on his hand. "Mad."

"They can be mad, but you need help. Y'all yellow." His face turned an angry red. "I'll get a job."

She was yellow? *Yellow?* "You're eleven. You need to stay in school."

"So?"

The sirens grew louder until it sounded as though they came from inside Misty's chest. George didn't leave her side. The smell of burning paper and melting plastic forced her focus over toward the kitchen. With beady eyes of judgment, their grandmother sat in the corner praying, worrying her beads and burning trinkets in a small porcelain dish. While Misty watched, she burned a photograph. After spitting on it. It was probably a photo of Misty.

George shook his head when he realized Misty was staring at their elder too. "She crazy."

"Demons inside!" Grandmother shouted, pointing at Misty.

"What is that? Who called them?" Misty's papa screamed as pounding erupted at the apartment door.

George scurried over to open it before anyone could turn them away. He'd be beaten for sure. Misty wondered if she died if they'd forgive George for letting the outside in.

Grandmother prayed louder, rocking. Mama stayed huddled in the kitchen while their papa tried to tell them everything was fine.

The paramedics entered, carrying their bags and a stretcher, ignoring everyone but Misty. The first paramedic who leaned down over her wore an expression of shock, then grave concern. He started asking her questions. There was a flurry of activity and Misty's pain softened. She tried to find George to tell him thank you, but she was whisked out of the apartment so fast she didn't see him again. Was this death?

CHAPTER FOUR

I'm that girl. *That's me.*

I didn't know if it was the bizarre ride behind the ambulance at speeds I'd never dreamed of . . .

Or if it was seeing that girl lifted out of the ambulance and rushed through silent doors into chaos . . .

Or if it was white coats hooking up machines, shouting, "Keep her going. Parents are on their way!" But one second I didn't know what was happening, and the next I knew I was watching my life from outside of myself.

I was the girl in the accident. My mask was gone. The lace camisole shredded until they totally removed it. My new jeans were cut off with careless shears.

It's kinda disorienting being on the outside.

Dark blood sprinkled and dripped into my newly pixied hair, making me look like an extra in a haunted house. But otherwise, a small, lumpy bruise on my forehead was the only visible mark on my body.

Questions rolled through my brain and I babbled at anyone within reach, but no one saw me, no one heard me, no one knew I was there . . . like the rest of my life . . . before.

The crowd dwindled until there was only one white coat and a few nurses in scrubs.

"Let's get this blood cleaned up before the parents get here."

"Stitches?" a nurse asked, peering at a gash on my head.

"Just bandage it." He shook his head. "Page me with any changes."

I kept floating toward the ceiling like a weird helium balloon, so I wrapped my legs around a nearby chair and held on. Gravity wasn't helping. I should have known something applicable from physics class last term, but all I kept thinking was: *Why am I out here? Am I dead? But I can't be dead because I wouldn't, or at least my body wouldn't, be in the hospital. Right?*

Several doctors, nurses, and kids not much older than me conferenced nearby. *Are those med students, maybe?* I tried to spacewalk my way toward them. They seemed to discuss me. At least, based on the pointing and sighing.

I'd maneuver closer, then be towed back toward my body. There was an unseen edge to this invisible world. A wall of maybe ten feet around the hospital bed kept me tethered nearby. In three directions, at least. *I'm not ready to try walking through walls.*

A nurse swooshed the curtain closed around my bed. I barely peeked at my body. I didn't like looking at myself in the mirror. Why should I look at me now?

It made me nervous.

I stopped when I heard the curtain rip.

Mother. *She looks like hell.*

Father was right behind her as if they'd arrived at the same time. It was his weekend alone with Carlton. Mine was next weekend. My brother was in his Spider-Man Halloween costume, face paint smeared like he'd been crying, or he'd wiped his snotty nose on the back of his hand. I scanned down his arms. Yep, paint decorated his hand. *Would the kid ever learn to use tissues?*

"Where's the doctor?" my mother demanded. "Why is she down here? We told you to put her in a private room." Mother's scathing tone was the one she used best, and most often, when she was nervous or upset. Straight from her gala, the black gown was wrinkled and the train torn as if she'd stepped on the dress in her hurry.

I'd really ruined her night and I was sure somewhere in her brain she was reformulating her lecture about "why couldn't I just be a normal cheerleader and happy with my life." She was probably asking herself, "Where did I go wrong to raise such an invisible mediocre student?"

"Mr. and Mrs. Chai, let's step into the conference room. Jane here will stay in the waiting room with your son while we talk." No longer covered in a white coat. This was the guy who basically called off everyone and said to tell him when the parents got here. He didn't seem to like me. *That can't be a good thing.*

"It's Ms. Carlton. We're divorced." Leave it to Mother to fluster the doctor for not knowing their marriage was over. The rest of us knew it. We couldn't get away from it. "We are not going anywhere until you tell us what happened."

"Oh. Sorry." With a nod to Jane, who asked Carlton if he liked candy and shuffled him away, the doctor repeated himself. "Oh. I'm sorry." He buried his head in my chart, made a few notes, then cleared his throat. "Your daughter has sustained a severe head injury."

"Like the soldiers coming back from war kind of traumatic brain injury? That'll take months to rehabilitate—" She was clearly calculating the hit to her social calendar with a daughter in rehab.

"No, ma'am, this is the kind of injury that is unrecoverable."

"She's not dead. She'd be in the morgue if she was dead. She's not dead, she's right here." Father pointed at my body, and the machine blew my chest up and down like a doll.

"I'm sorry to inform you, but the severity of her injury has left her brain-dead. We did everything we could, but right now it's machines keeping her body going. Without them, she is deceased."

"Why? Why put her on machines if she's dead? She's in a coma, right? People wake up from comas all the time. She'll wake up," Mother argued, her face draining of color until it was an inhuman shade of gray.

"She's dead? She's dead?" Father just kept repeating it over and over again.

The doctor didn't know who to listen to: Father's pacing, rambling repetition or Mother's bitch-like interrogation. He settled on Mother.

"She can live for a very long time with mechanical help. However, she is not going to wake up. Her body systems will shut down without the interventions."

Stopping near the head of my bed, Father said, "What happened to her hair?" he focused on my head. "Was that cut in the accident?"

"No, Richard, I told you on the phone she wanted to help sweet little girls with cancer."

"By cutting her hair?" His tone and expression were as perplexed as I'd ever seen them. Mother thought she made perfect sense and Father never quite understood her.

How many times had my parents spoken past each other? I had never felt bad for my father before, but now I saw him desperately trying to understand how my hair might cure cancer. As if that was easier to unravel than my imminent death.

I was numb. If I thought about the whole situation, I actually wasn't upset. *Is this shock? Do dead people go into shock too?*

"What happens now?" Mother asked, deflating into a chair near the bed. She was probably arming her next set of questions to lob at the doctors like grenades.

"You can take all the time you need." The doctor closed the chart and I knew he thought his bit part in this was over. *Not so fast.*

"Then what? We unplug her?" Father asked, frowning.

"That's a myth, sir, we don't literally unplug anyone. However, there are options you need to discuss with Nurse Brady."

Mother's eyes narrowed. "Why can't *you* discuss them?"

"Nurse Brady is our procurement coordinator—"

As if cued from offstage, a tall man with blazingly white hair and beard turned the corner and stepped forward. "Mr. and Mrs. Chai, I am so sorry for your loss. You have our deepest condolences." The man who might have been Santa Claus at the mall wore bright green scrubs and a jacket.

"It's Carlton. My last name is Carlton." Mother couldn't help herself. She patted my hand and dismissed him as irrelevant with a toss of her head. She began listing all the things I was supposed to do: homecoming, graduation, summa cum laude at a women's college, career, wedding, babies. The list continued getting more and more outlandish, more and more detailed.

"Procurement? Where have I heard that before?" Father asked. "Like, organ donor? But how?"

The nurse smoothly murmured apologies and kind words but how could he possibly know what my parents were going on about? "Why don't we step into the conference room for a little more privacy." He didn't ask, even though it was a question. His tone quietly demanded attention while still seeming sympathetic.

They nodded. Slowly shuffling in a daze behind him.

I had to hear this conversation. He herded them away and I went too, following along until I hit that invisible wall and was ripped back to the perimeter of the bed. To my body. *Let me go!* I strained, tried to listen, tried to scoot the wheeled bed across the room, but once they rounded the corner I heard nothing.

A doctor made notes on my chart, different numbers, different words than the others had marked down.

Yet a different woman in scrubs marched in and asked, "Should I page the team?"

"I don't know yet. These don't seem like parents who will see the ramifications."

"If only they knew patients were waiting—"

"Let Brady handle it. It's his job to educate them on donation."

"I don't know how he does it." She shook her head.

"Me either. Let's make sure we're not missing anything, though, so she's ready if they give the okay."

"You know we're not getting a miracle awakening on this one."

"Damn it all, kids are the hardest."

"Don't I know it."

Donation? Money to the hospital? To make me well? Didn't the doctor call Nurse Brady a procurement coordinator? What did he do? Father said 'organ donor,' as if they connected. I needed organs? Procurement? He is a Professional Cure doctor? To cure me? *Or no. . . . Think, Jessica. Think.*

NO! I screamed, leaping at my body, trying to force myself back inside. To open my eyes. To talk. To live. Donation? I wasn't meant to be served up. I AM HERE. YOU CAN'T JUST TAKE MY PIECES!

You can't make me.

CHAPTER FIVE

No, you can't do this. *I won't let you take me apart.* I tried to straddle the gurney covering my body with my . . . *my what? What or who am I now? Wake up, Jessica. Wake up now!*

Nurse Brady, aka Nurse Scalpel, and several others wheeled my gurney, machines, and beepers down the hall. My parents followed and they slid us into a private room.

"Take all the time you need." Nurse Scalpel moved away from us, his hands full of signed forms and my chart. I saw a brief glimpse of both of my parents' signatures.

I sent him a glare that I hoped made his ass pucker and his nose itch forever.

My parents said no. They had to say no. *Of course they said no. They'll wait for me to wake up.* They were the most selfish people on the planet, they were not going to let anyone cut me up and ship me around the world. Scalpel moved me out of the emergency room because they were going to wait for me to wake up. *That's it exactly.*

"She looks like she's sleeping so peacefully." Mother patted my hand and tapped her eyes with a tissue. *Ever afraid to run her mascara lest she be caught untended by someone she knows.* I wanted tears, ugly sobs of grief.

"She's not sleeping, Madeline."

Mother shot Father a pointed glare that felt eerily familiar. *I guess I know where I got that expression.* "I know that, Richard."

"I'm sure they need us to move this along," he said, ignoring her while digging in his pockets.

"Are you sure she's not in any pain?" Mother turned toward Father as if truly needing his reassurance. For a moment I saw the bonded trust that must have been there when they'd first married.

"They showed me the amount of pain meds in her system. She's not feeling anything." Father cleared his throat. He shredded an old gum wrapper into tiny silver confetti. It littered the floor unnoticed. "We should say good-bye and get out of here."

Where are we going?

"He said take my time. She's my baby." Mother turned away, toward me, and studied my face as if she saw me for the first time. "She was such a giving child."

I was? *When?*

Father nodded, but didn't speak.

"She thought she was going to change the world," Mother continued, weaving a brand-new story about my life.

"I'm sure she would have." Father sounded like he believed her, believed in me. But then he spoiled the moment by pulling out his phone and unlocking the screen.

"You can't have that on in here," Mother shrieked.

"What's the worst that can happen?" He spit back the words. *And we're back to normal.*

"She changed the world. She had plans." Mother stroked my hair, above the Band-Aid, where the nurse tried to sponge off all the blood until my blond looked orange. I wanted to grab Mother's hand and force her to stop touching me.

I did? When? Who are these people? Do they know nothing about me? Anything?

"We're doing the right thing, aren't we?" Father didn't glance up from his phone but his voice cracked.

Of course you are. I will wake up. I tried thrusting myself into my body. Again. I clicked my heels three times. I tried to do acrobatics and scream and sing and get someone's, anyone's, attention. I tried to pinch myself. Anything. Everything.

But I had no mass, no body, no nothing.

Nurse Scalpel returned and hovered at the door. "When you're ready," he said, before whispering to another nurse, who came in and checked the monitors, made notes, and added something to my IV bag.

Mother stood. "Carlton should say good-bye."

"He's too young," Father argued weakly, as if he knew he'd lose anyway.

"No, he's not."

Just until I wake up, right? A "see ya later"?

In a moment, Nurse Scalpel brought my little brother into the room. Carlton looked at once like a baby and an old man. I sensed he understood better than either of my parents what was going on.

"She's dead, isn't she?" he asked, reaching out to touch my toes but then stopping. His snotty, painted fingers retreated into knots behind his back.

You can touch me, Carlton. Touch me! Maybe I'll open my eyes and hug you back. Please.

"Yes," Father answered. "But she is going to help other people live." *Father? I'm here. Right here. What happens to me?* When Phinny my goldfish died, you told me there was no heaven. No hell. That it was a bunch of lies people told themselves because they were afraid. That he'd rot in the sewer system. I had nightmares for weeks in first grade.

And now? Now I'm terrified. Will you flush me too?

Carlton nodded, his bottom lip held between his teeth. He was trying not to cry.

Won't anyone cry?

A nurse plunged another syringe of something into my IV. I felt dizzy and tired.

"I'm not ready. I can't do this." Mother leaned across the bed. I lay down next to her. Next to me. Too exhausted to keep floating, too scared to try anything else.

"They need to take her, Madeline." Father cleared his throat again.

"What's going on? Where are they taking her?" Carlton asked.

If I'm here, I can't be dead, can I? Where's the tunnel? The light? Why, if there is no such thing as souls, am I still here? Explain this to me, Father!

Father answered. "They are going to harvest her organs now for other kids who need them."

"Like at a farm?" Carlton questioned.

"Yes." Father nodded.

"No." Mother sobbed.

"She's really dead?" my brother repeated as my father wrapped his hands around my mother's upper arms and lifted her off the gurney.

They ignored him. *Someone answer my brother!* I didn't want him to have nightmares about me rotting on some farm somewhere with corn growing from my eye sockets.

When it was clear our parents were too involved to listen, to even hear my brother, Nurse Scalpel knelt and met Carlton's gaze. "Jessica was driving a car and got in an accident. She hit her head really bad and her brain got hurt."

"Like a sprained ankle?"

I almost laughed. Thanks to gym class last week, and his lack of coordination, Carlton knew exactly what a sprained ankle was.

"Did you have a bum ankle? After a few days did it start to feel better?" Nurse Scalpel didn't break eye contact.

"Yeah, it's green but I'm not limping anymore. Wanna see?"

"Nah, I believe you." Nurse Scalpel continued, "Well, Jessica's brain can't get better. It was so hurt, it stopped working."

"But she's breathing like she's sleepin'."

"When she arrived at the hospital, we didn't know how badly her brain was hurt, and so we gave her machines to help her breathe, and keep her heart beating, until we knew if her brain could get better. But it stopped working and can't heal."

Carlton scrunched up his face. "Why keep the machines going?"

"There are lots of sick kids who need help to get better. And Jessica is going to be able to help them with transplants of organs and tissue she can't use anymore."

"Like bone marrow? My friend Evan's sister needed one of those and they couldn't find anyone, so Evan had to do it. He said it didn't hurt very much. Is it going to hurt?" His bottom lip trembled and his chin quivered.

"No, I promise it won't hurt."

"She really can't get better?"

"No, Carlton, she's dead."

"Okay, then she'd want to help the other kids like Evan's sister." Carlton's relief was profound and complete. He wouldn't have nightmares now. He understood.

"Good." Nurse Scalpel nodded in all seriousness, as if Carlton's questions were the most important ones of the day. In that moment, I loved this stranger for doing what my parents couldn't, or wouldn't, do for their son. He did the job I always took on, explaining things and answering Carlton's queries. *Who will do that now? I'm really dead?*

They began to wheel the gurney out of the room and down a long white hallway. *Is this the tunnel?* I felt myself drifting down the hallway, and then I fell asleep.

Or did I finally die?

SIX MONTHS LATER . . .

CHAPTER SIX

Samuel glanced up at the map he'd tacked to his bedroom wall. Twelve states down, thirty-six left, but the farther he researched away from New Mexico, the lower the odds of finding clues. Kidneys had a shelf life. He had to be there in the papers somewhere.

She. I'm a she.

Along the walls of maps in his current bedroom, pins and colored thread wove a web of intricate patterns I didn't understand, but Samuel seemed to interpret them as easily as most people recognized the smell of home.

Since day one, Samuel wasn't willing to let the time pass. And to him, the protocol of letting UNOS coordinate communication between donors and recipients seemed old-school and antiquated. He needed answers. He needed to know how his prayer was answered. Not in two years. Today. He worked his way out in ever larger circles. With Samuel's PRA count, his donor could have been anywhere within the United States. His kidneys and pancreas were rare, his tissue typing almost impossible to find.

Now he has mine and he's wasting them. I wanted to shake him and make him do something else. Anything else. Rather than spend his days trying to piece together the story of my death.

This kid has read three thousand, eight hundred, and forty-two obituaries and articles about fatal car accidents, drownings, and fires. How is he not killing himself from self-induced depression?

I tried to pick up a pen or type on the keyboard, anything, something, to save me from this agonizing search for the dead donor. *It's me! It's me!* Shouting, I jumped up and down, but he didn't hear me. I obviously didn't read enough paranormal novels to understand how ghosts got things done. Add that to the list of things I wish I'd done more of. *It's an impressive list and I'm only six months dead.*

I tried to hit the Return key again.

Bing!

I did it!

Craptastic, no, I didn't. That was the dryer downstairs signaling Sam's tighty whities were clean, and skid-mark free, at least, I hoped. I was forever scarred by that first day doing laundry with Sam.

Sam needed a break. He'd make himself nuts hunting up the Good Samaritan any longer today.

We heard his mother's footsteps, heavy on the floorboards, approach. I didn't understand their dynamic yet.

"Honey? Why don't you go to a movie? Or meet some friends to skateboard?" Sam's ma called tentatively through his closed bedroom door.

"Because I can watch movies in my room and I don't have friends or a skateboard. I don't know anyone here anymore," Samuel muttered under his breath. Too many months and years of chasing specialists and miracles from new hospital to new hotel and back. He closed his eyes and whispered, "You thought you'd get a normal boy, a real boy, when I got new organs, didn't you?" After a deep breath, and loud enough his ma heard, he said, "Maybe in a little while; I just have a couple more lines of code to drop in and then sure, I'll go outside."

"Okay, honey." We felt her waver.

I knew that tone. That was the tone of parents-who-don't-understand-their-kids-and-are-disappointed-by-the-reality-of-parenthood. I knew it well.

"Who's online?" Samuel's fingers flew over the keys and I plunked myself onto his bed. He wasn't going anywhere. Not soon. Or maybe at all. I knew this. I knew he placated his mom with promises and she let him. It was their thing.

"New message," he read aloud, but he didn't have to; if Samuel read it, saw it, thought it, I knew it too. And I have to admit that there are a few things I'd much rather unsee or unthink.

"'Yo, MiracleMan, I'm stuck on level six. Help.' Typical. Figure it out." Samuel didn't have patience for shortcuts. Not that I blamed him. Years plugged into machines had the power to turn even the most positive person into a bitter bossy-pants.

I started counting the glow-in-the-dark stars on his bedroom ceiling. His mother stuck them up while he was recovering from the transplant surgery. As if he were still eight. I'd only ever gotten to three hundred and six before my attention wandered. I had time. No rush.

The next message sat him straighter, tugged closer to the screen, as if that were possible, and frowning. *Not his usual.*

I moved behind him to see for myself.

MM—

Do you ever think miracles are just someone else's tragedy? Can they really be miraculous?

        —Misty

Samuel chewed his bottom lip and his fingers fluttered above the keys like they did when he was thinking hard. I think my response would be "good question," and leave it at that. This one struck him hard, and I wasn't sure why. I knew Misty too. I avoided her. But how did she find Samuel? Another link in the chain. Another thread in the web? *Snap out of it, Jessica.* Sam tapped out his words and sat, hovering above the keyboard.

Misty—

Every tragedy is someone's miracle. Why focus on the negative?

        —Samuel

He sat there staring at the screen for, like, ten minutes before he hit Send. *Boys. That's not what she was asking. I think.*

When Sam let himself be consumed hunting up other possible donors, I closed my eyes.

Maybe I should check on Misty? She makes me feel icky. I frowned. *Am I allowed to not understand her? Am I being a bad donor?* Today, I didn't care.

What's Vivian up to?

Vivian it is . . .

Vivian checked the levels of stock in the pencil trays. They were out of dark charcoal again. What was the big draw for charcoal pencils this month? Someone had to be taking them without paying. She'd mention it to Jackson before she left for the day. Her stomach rumbled. When did she eat last?

"Don't you have an exam to study for?"

Vivian turned toward Cassidy and shrugged. "I should, I guess." The thought of wasting time on memorizing geography appalled her.

"That class is a killer." Cassidy shook her head and moved off to help a customer.

"Yeah, but no one died from failing an exam." Vivian frowned.

Cassidy was normal. She worried about things like getting a date for Friday night and what college her parents could afford to send her to.

Life was slightly different for Vivian. I sighed. She worried about living to college age or if she was getting enough nutrition in her food or starving to death slowly because of the CF. Cystic fibrosis. *Yeah, just slightly different.*

"Excuse me?"

I should have known. He'd been thinking about art an awful lot lately.

Leif Leolin in an art supply store. *Will wonders never cease? He's gutsier than I gave him credit for.*

Vivian looked up into eyes the color of lime zest (Pantone 7737) or maybe they were pure grass green (Pantone 15-6437). She knew those eyes, she studied him every time they passed in the halls. Senior star with tragic story—Vivian knew exactly who he was.

Figure out the color later! Stop staring at him and say something. I wanted to blush in embarrassment for her. *Speak, darn it!*

"Uh, hello?" he repeated.

Vivian blanched before turning a brilliant shade of red. *I wonder what Pantone color you are now, Viv?* I felt a grin spread across my heart. I wondered if she felt it in a flutter. "Oh, can I help you?"

Leif slouched, his hands deep into his pockets, and rolled back on his heels. I knew he was nervous and completely shocked by the nerve it took to walk into the store. Once inside, he even forgot what he thought he wanted.

"Are you looking for a gift?" Vivian set her box down and started toward the gift-set section assuming, wrongly, that Leif was there at someone else's request.

"Uh, no." Leif pointed toward the watercolor crayons. "What are those?"

Vivian paused and changed direction, recalculating. She recognized the curiosity and spark of delight in Leif's eyes. "Let me show you."

CHAPTER SEVEN

Misty slid the mailbox key into the slot and pulled out the usual daily stack of bills. More doctors she didn't know were present in her crisis. More surgeons who were there at the hospital during those dark days. More medications she had to take or else. Everyone needed, no . . . wanted, a piece of her. Their share of dollars she didn't have. Her parents didn't have. Despair choked her.

The hall light was out again. Smoke from apartment 3B's daily burned meal coated the back of Misty's throat. The stairs reeked of dog poop and old garbage. Unfortunately, the tiny apartment her family shared didn't smell better, or appear much brighter, on the inside. There was nothing homey about her home.

Misty paused outside the apartment door. Was Papa laid off? Did he keep his job, his measly insurance? Or were the rumors true? Foreign-born workers, even legal ones, were always the first to go.

I hated it here. The smells of humanity living on top of each other. The desperation that seeped from everything. I wanted to shower and forget Misty lived like this. I knew she wanted to forget too. The start of voices arguing forced me back a step. I didn't want to hear this. Misty stepped forward.

If there was better insulation in the walls, maybe any in the door, Misty might have been forced to press her ear against the metal to hear bits of the conversation going on inside. As it was, all she had to do was stand outside; the yelling was easily decipherable, even in highly accented English. Misty didn't understand much of her parents' native language; she refused to acknowledge it on the grounds that her grandmother refused to learn English. So some of the words were impossible to understand for either of us, but the tone was crystal clear.

I cringed. No one needed to speak the language to know they were at it again. Ear-splitting curses, table-pounding fists, and shouted demands. Every time I was here, I left depleted.

Misty wilted further inside herself with each screech. Their neighbors came and went, stepping around her, paying no attention to the commotion behind the walls. Scenes like it seemed to populate every floor of this building. *No wonder she lives at the library on Aston and Edison.*

". . . she's your daughter too . . ."

An overused and obviously useless argument by Misty's mother.

"How are we supposed to feed the family . . ."

"They never should have talked us into allowing the surgery. . . ."

She would have died without the transplant, you idiots.

"How am I going to find work that pays enough?"

". . . insurance will lapse . . ."

Misty listened to every word with her eyes closed and her face blank.

Her crazy grandmother shouted encouragement and frankly egged on the fighting. I felt as if this family was spiraling down the drain with Misty caught in the undertow. With a choked sob, Misty stuffed the mail into her backpack and turned away from the apartment. She headed for sanctuary, and even I relaxed when her feet hit the pavement and left the screaming behind.

Once on Aston Boulevard, Misty used the little-known side entrance and returned the security guard's wave. They knew her here. No one knew her name, but book people recognized themselves in others and accepted her presence among them. It was as if everyone here understood that covers told them nothing about what happened inside.

Misty kept her head down and wove through the white marble pillars in the grand lobby of the Carnegie Library. Used by several independent colleges in the area, and as a public facility, it cradled the love of words with majestic stained glass and rich, gleaming wood. No chrome, or plastic, or beveled glass. It smelled of yesterday's lessons and tomorrow's promises.

The more time we spent here, the more I felt the humble and special appeal it held for Misty. There was peace here. Answers.

Between college kids with their gadgets and tomes of research, and the white-haired before-tech-ers who read printed newspapers and played games of chess, Misty glided silently back toward the historical biography section. Up a short, almost hidden, flight of stairs until she found a landing and the bank of computers she considered her own special place.

Dropping her backpack on the ground, she slid into a massive leather armchair that was surprisingly comfortable. She kept her hood up and her face buried in its folds. She had three more massive volcano zits along her jawline. She sighed, shifting in her seat as wispy fingers of ache filtered up her ribs and under her abdominal scar.

Logging in, she opened up her email inbox to see if Miracle-Man had responded. There were two messages. I felt her surprise. As if she thought her email would be as unwanted by him as her presence was at home. Hope was all she had left and it fluttered faintly. She read his first message and she flipped off the screen in frustration. Think positive? Why was that everyone's stupid advice?

But then she opened his second message:

> Hi, M——
>
> I sounded like a dumb fortune cookie before. Sorry. Jackass.
> What's your story?
>
> —Samuel

Misty's lips twitched with the tiniest smile as she reread his message ten times. "Total dumb fortune cookie." Did he understand? Could he?

Better than you think he might. Write him back! I wondered if I was the only one of us to recognize the much needed lifeline he'd tossed her.

But what was her story? What would she say to him? Would she be honest? I waited, holding my metaphorical breath.

Her screen blinked and there was a messaging request. She clicked for info. "Who is it?"

Samuel aka MiracleMan. Ah, good job, Sammy!

"Wanna chat?" Misty read out loud. Did she? What did he want? What was his angle? Without overthinking it, Misty clicked on the blinking icon.

```
M: hi
S: sorry
   again
M: it's ok
S: whyd u ask?
```

Why had she asked a stranger? The Internet's *Daily Miracle* newsman. Misty pictured an old guy, like a loony professor in a suit and never-combed hair. The cursor blinked at her. Waiting.

```
M: thought u might no
S: the mystery is inherent in the miracle
   otherwise theyd just be normal stuff
   or maybe the normal stuff is the miracle
```

A wave of intense dizziness squeezed the breath out of Misty's lungs. Her vision grayed. She breathed through it. Forcing her feet to feel the insides of her shoes, the carpet beneath. Insisting her brain register that she still sat in the armchair. But her fingers curled off the keys and her ears rang with internal screams. The cursor mocked her.

```
S: misty?
S: misty?
S: come in MISTY?
```

Come on, Misty, talk to him. He cares.
Misty blinked back tears. Weariness laid heavy hands on her shoulders and shoved her deeper down. She slid bonelessly

toward the earth. Under the far desk caddy, beneath the Russian poets and surrounded by theologians' and philosophers' lives etched in words.

Misty huddled in her sweatshirt, tucking her knees against her stomach. No one saw her. No one used this section. She closed her eyes and forced herself to find a place where she felt safe. It was there. Somewhere deep and far down in the dark.

CHAPTER EIGHT

Vivian saw Leif staring up at one of her most recent pieces, hung high on the studio wall. Mathilda No-last-name. She knew the portrait of this one-hundred-year-old homeless lady was haunting and disturbing. It drew viewers in and didn't let them go. People either loved it or hated it. Curiosity stroked her forward.

"Hi," she said, approaching cautiously. Why was he back again today?

Because art is in his blood, he just doesn't see it yet. And he likes you. I grinned.

"How'd they do this?" he asked, without looking directly at her.

A common question that no one really wanted details about. "Bunch of different kinds of paints. Layered. Blown through various diameter pipes and straws." Vivian shrugged before she gave herself away.

"Really?" Leif frowned, as if he was thinking about arguing.

Great, Leif, you sound like she's making stuff up and you don't believe her. Way to woo a girl. I wanted to smack his shoulder, but settled for rolling my eyes. At least thinking I did.

Since it was her work, Vivian felt very comfortable answering him with a smile and incredulous expression. "Really."

"Oh, sorry, that sounded rude, didn't it?" Leif rubbed his knuckles. "I've just never seen anything like it. I wanna do that." He pointed.

"That's, um, difficult to do—" Vivian broke off. How was she going to explain the years it took to master these techniques? She didn't want to discourage him, but he wouldn't off the bat be able to paint portraits full of mini pictures—definitely not with blowing. Maybe on the computer with Photoshop. *And plagiarism.*

"I don't m-mean . . . obviously . . . I m-mean," Leif stuttered. He stopped staring up at the picture, then focused his gaze on his hands while blood crept up his neck. Finally, he made eye contact before his gaze flitted away from hers. He was a doofus when he got nervous. She seemed to like it, though. *I didn't understand why Vivian's heart continued to tizzy and surge, but whatever.* "Can you show me what to do? I mean, what do I use to, uh, 'blow,' you said?" His face flushed.

These two spend more time blushing than talking.

"Now?" Vivian expected him to lose interest and move on. Go back to the gym instead.

"Yeah, can you?" His face lit up.

"Sure." Part of her job was demonstrating and helping customers with their work, she did this all the time for others. Why did showing Leif seem more intimate and personal? "We'll start easy."

She headed toward the back of the studio space. Several painters worked with music blaring only in their ears, others chatted with each other. This wasn't the place to work as a loner who didn't like people.

Leif followed. "Do you, uh, blow?"

Good god, Leif.

"Paint, blow paint," he corrected, but Vivian didn't even acknowledge the double entendre of his words.

Girl needs to watch some Showtime. Mistake #1 for Jessica Chai— thinking there'd always be a next time.

"Yeah, I know the technique." She stopped at that.

Why? Tell him that's yours up there on that wall! Tell him people pay you thousands of dollars to blow. Please? I want to see his expression.

"Cool." Leif nodded.

In instructor mode, Vivian commandeered a workstation. "We'll start with scrap paper and watercolors. It'll give you a feel."

"Sure . . . sure," Leif answered.

Vivian prepared paints and straws while Leif wandered, observing the other artists. She and Leif obviously struggled for conversational topics any time they were within each other's range. When she was ready, she motioned him over. "The key is to really just play with how hard you exhale and point the straw in the direction you want the medium to go. Don't inhale the paint."

"Can you show me?" Leif looked like a lost little boy.

"Yeah." Vivian demonstrated several times, making it look astoundingly easy.

"You're really good at this." Leif was impressed.

Cassidy heard him and cracked up as she went by, carrying fresh canvases.

"What?" Leif frowned. "What'd I miss?"

Vivian shook her head, trying to get Cassidy's attention.

"That's her painting." Cassidy pointed at the lady's portrait. "Oh, so is that one. And that one just sold to a guy in Iman or Iran or—"

"United Arab Emirates. Thanks, Cassidy." Vivian swallowed.

"Oh, that's right. No problem." Perky and undisturbed, Cassidy returned to the front of the store.

Leif froze in his chair. His leg fidgeted under the table. He hated feeling stupid.

Vivian hated the ugly silence (Pantone 3985) that wedged between their chairs.

"I'm sorry," Vivian apologized, to break the silence. "I don't know how to tell people about my work. I don't want to sound like I'm showing off, or make anyone feel like they need to compare." She stammered, trying to find words for the colors she felt. "I was afraid—"

"I get it. It's not like I ever greeted the crowds with a list of my stats. It could be interpreted as rude."

Vivian sighed. "Yes, exactly."

"You're amazing. I m-mean, your work is—" Leif stuttered.

I'd always assumed he was smooth and born to flirt until I watched him in action.

"Thanks. Here, try this color." Vivian handed him a tube of slightly thicker paint in a purple that could almost be called blue.

He took the switch of paints and they worked in comfortable companionship. I envied people who could sit side by side and not speak, not feel the need to fill the void. Eventually, Vivian grabbed ice-cold bottles of water from the fridge and handed him one.

Leif's painting looked like one of those the elephants at the zoo did with their trunks. Only his had a layer of sprayed spit. "That's like trying to inflate a balloon made of tire rubber." He gestured at the last blob of acrylic yellow. "How did you get started?"

Vivian paused, wondering how honest to be. She didn't want to lie to Leif, but part of her questioned if he wanted the real story or the sanitized version. She headed for the middle of both. "My dad. I needed a lot of lung therapy as a kid. I had a cough and bronchitis a lot. But I hated it all." *Nice understatement. Make the therapy sound like taking out the trash instead of a necessary brutality.* "When I was little, I played with my food. He made it into a game with me blowing peas down the dining room table. He made me graduate to grapes quickly, then shampoo, pudding, oranges—if it could move or roll, he put it in front of me." *Leave out the coughing and hacking up tons of sticky phlegm and it almost sounds fun.*

Leif nodded, sipping his water and listening closely. I knew his casual facade belied the pointed energy he listened with.

"One day, he was watching one of those kid craft shows." *The kind that are on during the day when you're stuck in the hospital with your sick kid.* "They were blowing paint for some place mat thing, I think. He thought he could get me to work my lungs harder if I was painting. I loved those paint-with-water books and my coloring books. It worked. I still use watercolors, but now I use all sorts of paints and viscosities."

Leif motioned her over to stand beneath Mathilda No-last-name again. "Is that how you get the depth like it's her real skin?

69

Using lots of different paint types?" He squinted up, studying the portrait so closely.

"Yeah, something like that." Vivian was relieved he didn't ask about her being sick or why she needed so much lung therapy. Healthy kids didn't understand CF and they seemed to fear an impossible contagion. She wondered what it would be like to have Leif study her that closely. Would he, could he, see beyond her outsides to the reality within?

"Wow. Cool." They moved back toward his workstation. He was enthused. He picked up the straw again and focused on the paper in front of him. Vivian watched his expression cloud and furrow. She knew this expression—she'd seen it often when her friends bore down to do physical therapy they knew hurt but had to be done. She didn't understand why he wore it, though. Painting didn't hurt.

"It just takes practice," she assured him as he blew along a dot of celestial blue (Pantone 19-4530).

He frowned, but replied, "Right. Okay."

"Hey, Viv, I need your help with this order," Cassidy called.

"I'll practice." He pulled his chair closer to the table and hunkered down as Vivian joined Cassidy at the front of the shop. Was this the expression he wore during a losing game? *Or a winning one?*

Hours went by under a crush of odd and complicated customers, and Vivian assumed Leif had left while she was busy.

Nope, check again, chica.

There were only thirty minutes until the close of the store and time to start straightening up for the weekend morning rush. Yep, she worked on Friday nights. Especially when she was healthy. It made her feel less awkward about having no social life. She blamed work to her family. She didn't know who, if anyone, believed her.

"You're still here?" She stopped in her tracks, seeing Leif bent over another piece of paper.

"I can't get it right."

Vivian moved closer, closing tubes and screwing on lids. She straightened up out of habit with quick and graceful movements. She stood over his table and saw the series of pages, clearly an evolution of attempts as he worked on a green line, topped it with a brown circle, and then began to add yellow petals. To her, his current page looked like a fairly perfect single sunflower. But if he was going for a dog, or a dolphin, he had a ways to go—she'd learned to be careful until she knew the artist's intent. Too many people burst into tears after hours of not transferring their vision to the page.

"It's a—?" She left the question dangling.

"Oh hell, it's supposed to be a flower. Is it that bad you can't tell?" Leif sank his head into his hands. Yellow paint speckled his forehead and a streak of green wove through his hair like a leprechaun highlight.

She rushed to reassure him. "No, no! It's good. It's great. It's just I wasn't sure what you meant to paint. I mean, you should see some of the bowls of fruit people paint in our classes that end up looking like a pile of vomit, or the nude drawings that look more like spiderwebs or robots than people. I mean, it's good—really good." Vivian knew she was rambling, but he looked so sad her heart hurt. Rejections of any kind hurt, even the unintentional ones. "This is your first time. And you're new to art, right?"

"Painting? Yeah. It's obvious?" Leif nodded as though she'd delivered a life-imprisonment sentence. As if he knew his happiness depended on something that would never work.

Vivian sat down. She reached out and touched her fingertips to his shoulder. Just the tips, but it took every ounce of mustered courage she had. She caught a whiff of spicy cologne and wanted to lean closer, but she didn't. "Only cuz you're so unsure of yourself. Really. It takes practice. You didn't score a touchup the first time you held a ball, right?"

Leif glanced up. "A what?"

Vivian blanched. "Sorry. Whatever you score in football." She licked her lips and shrank back against the chair before standing. She'd used up all her courage.

Leif started laughing. "A touchdown." He laughed harder. "No, I guess I didn't."

Stop laughing, she thinks you're laughing at her. I wanted to smack him.

"Um, I need to close up." Vivian tossed the empty water bottles into the recycling without making any eye contact.

"Oh, sorry." He jumped to his feet, almost pushing the chair over. Vivian saw him flinch as if his leg didn't want to hold his weight, but she didn't point it out. He hid it quickly and she assumed he didn't want her to notice. *He doesn't.* "I'll be out of here in no time. I guess I'll just toss these away?" he asked, looking for a garbage can to throw away his dry and half-dry paintings.

"I'll do it," Vivian answered briskly.

"No, no, I'll clean up my stuff." Leif didn't understand why she'd gone all frosty on him.

She paused. "It's okay."

Good grief, these two give me a headache. Neither of them wanted to leave. *So don't!*

Leif tried to extend an apology, though he had no idea what he'd done. "You wanna get coffee?"

"I have to stay here and finish up—"

"Oh, right. Sure." He picked up his bag and backed away, almost running over an easel.

Don't let him leave. Say something.

"You like breakfast?" Vivian blurted.

"Breakfast?"

"I have to work at ten, but the best omelets and cinnamon rolls are served next door."

Leif grinned. "I love breakfast."

Vivian returned his smile. "Good. Say eight-thirty?"

"Yeah, see you tomorrow." Leif waved on his way out the door.

She sank into a chair, and how long she stayed frozen I'm not sure, but my heart pounded so hard I thought perhaps she was going to break it. The thundering didn't stop until long after Leif's scent dissipated and the door swung shut behind him. I wanted to tell her it was soap and deodorant, but she wouldn't have listened.

"I asked Leif Leolin out. I asked Leif Leolin out." Vivian kept repeating this to herself in a breathless whisper full of shock and disbelief.

Technically, he asked you out and you responded after shooting him down.

"I mean he asked first, but I didn't say no totally." Vivian finally felt her legs again and stood up. "Where did I get the courage?"

73

Don't look at me. I never asked a boy out, not a first time, or in retaliation.

Vivian smiled through the rest of her cleanup, and I didn't need to hang around to know who she'd be dreaming about tonight.

CHAPTER NINE

Samuel untangled the power cords and took his homemade laptop outside. Ma played old hymn records so loud he was sure she thought God himself might sing along. The late spring sun was warm, but low clouds flowed continuously over the sun like a newsfeed on the bottom of the screen. Was Earth God's reality television? What was His endgame and prize? Who was His target audience? Who did the casting?

I wasn't sure God cared about any of us, or if there even was a God. Maybe that's why I was still here. My parents taught an uninspired lack of faith, while Samuel's ma was so over-the-top that I hoped truth lay in between. Sam read about religions and works by people like the Dalai Lama, Billy Graham, and Rabbi Shimon Finkelman the way Vivian saw the world through colors. His faith used to be unwavering, but recently I'd started to feel questions rising. But maybe it was just me. *Maybe I question too much?*

Sam flicked through news sites, searching for the latest miracles. Anything was game. He posted video clips, links to websites, photographs, and stories. His definition of miracle was the importance he wanted people to notice. From the list of comments and the constant flow of incoming messages, the number of people who paid attention to his site grew every day.

There was a story about a double amputee who successfully summited Mount Everest and another about a kindergartner who hand-raised kittens after she watched a man toss them into a Dumpster. A frog, born without a back leg, living happily in Boston's garden conservatory, was adopted as the mascot for local Special Olympians. Samuel's list grew as he weighed the pros and cons of possible posts. Hours he used to spend in dialysis. This was how he filled the other hours of the day. The hours not filled with the hunt for me.

All Samuel wants is for people to wake up and see the world around them. And to participate in their own lives.

He most often posted things about people choosing to do the hard thing, the right thing, rather than taking the easiest path. The unemployed person who returned a full briefcase of savings bonds to a widow. The child who started a school turkey drive because her best friend had never had turkey at Thanksgiving. Parents of a dying three-day-old girl who gut-wrenchingly fought grief by donating her organs and subsequently saved five other babies, five other sets of parents from burying an infant. Sam liked the stories that made people aware that they could choose to alleviate suffering rather than contribute to it.

Though he tried to hide and ignore her, his ma tracked him down, waiting only a few heartbeats before launching. "Samuel, Mrs. Wayland's son, Trevor, has invited you to his birthday party on Friday night."

Not another friend date. Samuel had barely healed before she'd begun thrusting him out into the world. Apparently anyone under the age of eighteen was a potential friend hookup for her only son. That's all her standards seemed to stop at—age. She'd invited more random boys over for cookies and milk than hard-core pedophiles.

"I have plans. And, isn't he ten?" Samuel didn't look up. He knew eye contact was an unfavorable idea.

She tsked so hard, spittle flew from her lips. "You don't have plans."

Gross. I tried to wipe my face clean on reflex.

"There's a gaming tourney this weekend. Starts Friday afternoon." Samuel rarely lied. But sometimes lying was the only way to get her to back off. *I don't understand why he even tries the truth. Just tell her what she wants to hear.*

"They're going camping up in the mountains, Samuel. It will be fun."

I watched her lock her knees and cross her arms. Sam clenched his jaw and hissed an inhale. I felt sorry for him.

"Why do you want me to go camping with a bunch of kids?" he asked.

She sighed. That sigh was never a good sign, even I knew that. "I want you to make friends."

"I have friends." His rapid-fire answer dismissed her. *Uh-oh.*

"Oh yes, your friends online? Invite them to dinner, I'd like to meet them. You can't, can you? They don't exist. They are not real people. Real friends come to dinner."

"Ma—"

"Don't take that tone. You are going camping with Trevor and his friends. I already said yes."

"I'm seventeen!" Sam shouted.

"Don't worry, Samuel. I'm sure some of those boys play games too." She turned on her heel back toward the house.

He paused and sat with it for a moment. Dammit. At least when he was on dialysis every day she couldn't force him to go camping. Camping? *Sam camping?*

He needed to charge up his extra batteries. What a pain in the ass.

Misty shifted in the seat again. Her bony butt felt bruised and sore from the hard chairs that populated her school days. She smothered a halfhearted yawn. She needed to get more sleep, or better sleep, or something.

Bell ring. Bell ring, please. School or apartment, Misty's life sucked.

I never wanted to return to high school, but there were days when I missed my life so much it was worth the pain. Someone needed to keep an eye on Misty even if I was the only choice.

Back in these halls it felt like Groundhog Day, a loop that made my skin crawl. I felt like I relived the trauma of that last school day over and over again. I kept waiting for someone to pop out at me in the hallways wielding scissors, but they couldn't see me. *Nothing changes. No one really sees Misty either.*

Misty's class schedule was a couple of levels down from mine in the world of the mediocre student. English. Math. Civics. State history. Art. PE. She cared about none of it. She only wished she could get paid to be there. Her locker was full of unpaid medical bills she hadn't felt good enough to log in yet.

The last bell rang and I jumped up, ready to get going. Misty needed the library's refuge. I knew this. Did she? Classmates disappeared like a magic act. Misty didn't move very quickly, so she was last to leave.

"Misty?"

Misty blinked before raising her eyes, but she avoided eye contact, fearful the teacher might see too much. "Yes, Mrs. Youngs?"

I knew that look. Misty wasn't going to be asked about an assignment. This was the caring, the I-notice-you teacher face. Nine out of ten times it wasn't like they really wanted a response; they just wanted to make sure that they'd asked, in case. Well, in case. In *my* case, there was a staff meeting the day I skipped school because someone reported the Skirts bullying me. I don't know who saw, or who spoke up, but it was too late. Obviously, because I died that weekend. The new school policy was to react faster. How? No one really knew. And if there were consequences for the Skirts for that assault, I didn't know that, either.

Mrs. Youngs leaned against her desk and folded her hands as if in prayer. "Misty, I am worried about you. Your grades have continued to slip and I have spoken with your guidance counselor. We want you to know that we're here for you. We've reached out to your parents but they haven't responded."

Panic raced through Misty's system. A hit of adrenaline. The tang of fear. The sudden twisting of her insides in rebellion.

Didn't they realize that there were things more important than grades?

Bigger than school?

Misty's brain locked up, blanked out, trying to think of something, anything, to say. I wanted to hug her. I wanted to choke the teacher.

That morning at the library, Misty had carefully opened the newest stacks of bills. She organized them by date, by doctor, by procedure. She marked the invoice numbers, the amounts paid and owed, the dates sweeping past like the hands of a clock. She tucked them into a box she hid behind the Russian poets, between the shelves, books, and back wall. Every bill, every letter demanding payment, she kept. That morning, the running tally of what her family owed, that went unpaid, topped a quarter of a million dollars. Her medications, follow-ups, and treatments might be a hundred thousand dollars a year. Forever. *There are no classes in how to keep track of medical bills and how to pay them with no job, no help. Misty might ace that class.*

I wondered if my parents got a bill for my brief, but high maintenance, time at the emergency room, in the operating room. Did they get a bill from the surgeon for taking all my pieces? Or in some karmic system did they get monetary credit for my sacrifices?

"I'm fine, Ms. Youngs. Still recovering from the liver transplant. They said it would take a while for me to focus and feel one hundred percent. I'm not supposed to push too hard. My parents work a lot." Misty's lie rolled off her tongue. I'd watched her use the words "liver transplant" enough to realize exactly what she wanted to accomplish.

Immediately, the teacher's posture changed. "I don't want to pressure you. I simply want you to know I am here if you need anything. Tutoring. Extra time after school. Whatever I can do."

Misty had insurance for a week before it ran out. Her parents didn't tell the doctors that it was ending. Billing didn't double check. A girl shouldn't see how much saving her life cost and the money it took to maintain. It's not something I ever thought about. What would you pay? You say anything? Did anything mean living in a hovel and eating beans out of food banks for the rest of your life? That no matter how hard you worked you'd never catch up, never make enough for a breath free from that crushing weight?

"Thank you," Misty said, hoping she might escape soon.

"You're a very brave, and very lucky, girl, Misty. I'm sure you know how proud we all are of you."

For getting sick? For having a dead person's organ? My liver inside her? What did she have to do with that? Why would either of those things make her brave?

Misty nodded and didn't let the door close before she put her head down and dove into the sea of flailing bodies in the hall. I was never sure where to look. At people I recognized? At people I'd never seen before because I used to stare at the tiles under my feet? At the banners and artwork and flyers that seemed like a hodgepodge of colors and demands?

I forgot Misty for a moment. Until she shuffled past a glass case.

That's me!

Within the glass walls was last year's yearbook photo blown up to poster size. Me. Generic blue background. Long hair pulled back in a braid snaking over my shoulder. My eyebrows so blond they seemed nonexistent. My mouth gave a Mona Lisa smile. It could be interpreted as happy, or secretive, or miserable, but it wasn't a tooth-baring grin.

Misty, stop. Please.

Misty leaned against the wall, grabbing my attention. They

never listened to me. They never did what I asked. My shrine forgotten for a moment, I studied her. She was sweating, cold, and clammy. Her heart raced and she inhaled shallow, panicked breaths. As she waited, I drifted back toward the case.

A few handmade We'll Miss You signs and drying roses that were molding in that plastic tumbler they sold at football games. There were two newspaper clippings and a couple of printed online bits. One was an article accompanied by this same photograph and—

Misty thrust herself forward. The ribbon, or force field, or whatever I called this invisible thing that tied us together, only stretched so far.

I want to see those clippings.

I need to read those pages.

Misty ignored me and continued on farther away.

Yes, six months had passed. I tried not to notice everyone walking around the case without glancing at it, let alone caring about the girl inside, but being ignored so quickly hurt. Was my life really that easily forgotten?

CHAPTER TEN

Leif's feet hit the pavement in an almost steady rhythm, with only the slightest hesitation on his right side. His knee ached, but it was so much less than it had been, he tolerated it fine. It was the stiffness in the morning he wasn't used to yet.

Another lap down. I've never understood people who run on a track. You're going in circles. By choice. Isn't that silly?

I wished a hungry tiger escaped from the zoo to chase everyone . . . at least then they'd have a reason to try to run faster. The circle part notwithstanding.

Leif's mind wandered. He worked on a "thing" in his head.

It's called a song. It's poetry put to music. Why does he insist on calling his passion for writing songs a "thing"?

In his head, a girl in a white nightgown waited at a window. The lyrics rhymed. He frowned, and the girl's dress shifted to jeans and a tank top.

Not any easier to rhyme, doofus. Plop. Mop. Crop. Wean. Mean. Seen. *I have a headache.*

As he worked, his pace picked up. When he blew through the start-finish line, he wasn't remotely paying attention to the world around him. The coach's whistle blew a shrill reminder and Leif ran back toward the herd of tracksters.

I continually found the amount of Lycra and bare skin on the girls at these practices astonishing. Leif's baggy, calf-length shorts and rotting plain T-shirt were the uniform for the boys. The girls all seemed to "shop in the easy department," if my mother's judgment wasn't too harsh.

Would I still be alive if I hadn't tried so hard to be good, boring, and bland for my entire life? Maybe if I'd worn Lycra earlier, once in a while, I wouldn't have gone to that stupid party.

The whistle tooted short bursts until the track team quieted. After debriefing the season, and talking about off-season nutrition and training, and maybe even how to train poodles—I was trying to get a bird to poop on the coach's head instead of paying attention—finally, the coach shouted, "Go hit the locker room and get ready for the awards ceremony. Your parents should be here and we'll get started within an hour. Circle up. Color chant on three. One. Two. Three."

As if one body with fifty voices they began, "Gold!"

"Black!"

"Who's got your back?"

"We got your back!"

"Black!"

"Gold!"

"Who's takin' first?"

"First is sold to black and gold." Applause, cheers, and whistles filled the stadium and echoed back as if the stands were full.

I'd never been much for chanting. But I thought Leif loved this team stuff.

He shouted the words with his team but they were empty. He used to get fired up and feel a part of something bigger than himself. It didn't matter that the cheer sounded as if it had been made up by a third grader, it was theirs. Now he only felt stupid.

Interesting. Poor Leif is starting to feel human.

As the sounds died down, Coach called out, "Leif, stay back. I want to talk to you."

"Sure, Coach." Leif watched his teammates jog off the track field. They chatted and joked and he stayed frozen on the grass, waiting for the coach to talk to him.

Coach put his arm around Leif's shoulders. It felt heavy and too tight, more like a yoke for oxen than a gesture of camaraderie. *My stomach tightened at Leif's surge of discomfort.*

Uh-oh.

Coach said in a low tone, like they were part of a conspiracy, "I want you to know how much we appreciate you working out with us this season. The freshmen got a look at a world-class teammate. Stellar commitment to sport. There will be a special new award tonight. Want you to take a few minutes and gather some thoughts to share."

Thoughts on what? Working out? Leif didn't have any words of wisdom.

"And I want you to know how much we appreciate your father's support of the booster program. Camp this summer will be possible for us because of his—"

Leif jerked away to face the older man. "Wait, what? My dad did what?"

"He made a sizable contribution to the athletic fund. I'm

sorry, son, I thought you knew." Coach shrugged as if it wasn't a big deal.

"No." Leif quickly shut down the expression on his face, but anger boiled in his gut. "Thank you." He was being given an award because his daddy wrote a check. Heaven forbid they show up at a sports-award ceremony and their kid doesn't get an honor. They made up an award for him. *Ouch.*

Coach continued obliviously. "We're calling it the 'No Quit' trophy. Looking forward to handing it to you."

Leif's hands fisted and he stepped farther away. His tongue felt swollen and obscene in his mouth.

The coach didn't notice as the local reporter called out to get the man's attention. "I'll see you later, son. Thanks again for showing us how to be a competitor."

Leif took his time getting to the locker room. With no witnesses, he leaned against the brick wall behind the gym and pounded it with his open palm until the skin burned and split. His parents would expect him to smile and take the applause. For doing what?

He wiped the sweat from his forehead.

He needs to leave.

He reached into his pocket and felt for his tiny MP3 player. He swished the volume up and pushed off the wall. He didn't have to be at the ceremony. Let them accept the bogus award.

I frowned. Leif lived for this kind of thing, didn't he?

He took off, racing around the back of the school until he hit the bike trails that circled our town.

I guess not.

He ran until blisters rubbed on his heels. He ran until his body dripped sweat as if he'd just come from a swim. He ran until there was nothing in his head. Nothing at all. As the sun began to set, Leif knew the awards banquet had to be about over, but he didn't want to go home. Not yet. His muscles burned and moaned with fatigue. Damned overachiever ran a marathon before noticing he overdid it.

I wanted to huff and puff and catch my breath too. I was beginning to forget what exercise felt like in my own body. I used to hate exercise. *Funny, the things we miss.*

He started walking the backstreets of town. The alley door to Art and Soul was propped open. He pulled his earbuds from his ears and heard country rock thump out at him. Was Vivian working?

You smell, Leif. Resist.

He sniffed himself quick and passed his truly impaired olfactory test.

I hope she really likes him.

He used his already-soaked shirttail to smear the sweat across his face before hesitating for a few heartbeats outside the door. What if she wasn't inside? What if she didn't want to see him? He stepped forward and turned a corner into a private studio space.

"Leif?" Vivian quickly turned her canvas away from the door and clicked off the music. "What are you doing back here? Are you okay?" Her expression went from shock to pleasure to concern in three blinks. She cataloged his expression as a dreary gray (Pantone 414).

He stepped side to side, as if testing his knee, then dropped into an empty chair. He hadn't noticed how exhausted his body was until he stopped moving.

"Are you thirsty? I'll get you water." She fled the room.

Will she come back?

She returned with her arms full of sweating plastic bottles. *Did she clean out the fridge?*

"Isn't track over?" she asked, handing him a couple of cold bottles.

"Thanks." Leif chugged one whole bottle before taking a breath and nodding. "Today was the debrief practice to talk about next year and summer training."

"Oh. Are you okay?" she repeated.

He stared at his hands. I saw how torn he felt. He wanted to talk. He wanted to confide in her, but his tongue flopped around without obeying.

"Sorry. Never mind." Vivian stiffened, and I knew she took his silence personally, like he didn't want to answer the question because she asked it.

Leif blurted, "My dad paid the coach to give me an award."

"I didn't think you were competing on the team." Vivian frowned but relaxed.

"I wasn't. Just working out as part of my physical therapy."

"Oh." Vivian sat down next to him. I hoped she was down-wind. "He can do that?"

Leif grinned ruefully and shook his head. "Yeah, he does whatever it takes to be number one."

"What's the award?"

"The 'No Quit' trophy."

"Oh." Vivian glanced away. I felt a giggle bubble up in her stomach. She tried to swallow it back but couldn't catch its tail. It dribbled out, breaking open her lips so more could follow. She slapped a hand over her mouth, trying to smother the giggles, but they just kept coming.

Leif looked at her in surprise.

Come on, Leif, you have a sense of humor, I know it. Laugh.

He chuckled, and that made her laugh more. Soon, they were both laughing so hard I thought they might split open their scars.

"Congratulations?" Vivian snorted out the word, which sent them both spiraling back into guffaws the joyous hue of sunshine (Pantone 108).

"Thanks." Leif swallowed more water.

They sat as silence gently blew in around them, until Vivian asked, "But isn't the banquet tonight? Like, now?"

"Yep. I'm skipping it." Leif's tone was steady and confident, with just a dusting of insecurity that maybe only I heard.

"Wow. That's brave."

Leif frowned. "No, it's not."

"Have you ever gone against your parents before?"

Leif shook his head. "No, I guess not." He'd always thought he wanted to be the best too. That winning was everything.

"Will they worry? When you're not there?" she asked.

He shrugged, standing up. His knee throbbed and tightened.

"You should text them that you're all right," Vivian pressed.

"Maybe. What are you working on?" Leif changed the subject.

"A new painting of a special girl."

He moved toward it. "Can I see it?"

Vivian blocked him with her body.

Leif raised his hands in surrender. "Not ready?"

"Not yet. Wanna come over? If you want to avoid going home. Are you hungry?" Vivian's voice drifted off as if she realized what and who she was asking. She'd never brought a boy home. It wasn't like a date.

Sure, Viv, keep telling my heart you aren't falling for Leif.

"Starved," he answered.

"How about pizza?"

"Awesome." Leif smiled and Vivian's body filled with bright violet (Pantone 19-3438).

CHAPTER ELEVEN

Vivian's mom took one look at Leif and ushered him into the guest bathroom along with a set of clean workout clothes belonging to her husband.

"Mom," Vivian hissed in embarrassment.

"He'll feel better cleaned up. Besides, you don't want to kiss a stinky boy. You want a fresh and clean kiss." Her mother's eyes twinkled and Vivian wanted to drop through the floor. Instead, she checked on their pizza order and studied herself in the hall mirror, listening for the sound of running water to stop.

Vivian saw a garden gnome staring back at her. With a full-moon face and puffy, short stature, she annually threatened to wear a gnome costume for Halloween. She never did because she was too afraid people would then always see her wearing a red, pointed hat, an old-fashioned dress, and wooden clogs. Not the "real" her.

Her dirty-blond hair went brown in winter, and because of the new antirejection meds, grew in thicker and fuller. Almost black at the roots, and it was so curly it frizzed with the least humidity. Her eyebrows needed trimming daily, and her skin was so prone to breakouts that she'd perfected concealer application. She turned away from her reflection. There was no way Leif would see anything desirable when he looked at her. No way.

I wanted to comfort her and tell her she was wrong. But I wasn't sure. He dated willowy, waxed, and highlighted girls with big boobs, tiny waists, and smaller IQs. Leif was such a jumble of conflicts.

Leif strode into the kitchen with a chagrined smile on his face. "Your mom was right. I needed that."

They chatted about Art and Soul, the latest music, even the weather, as they tried to dance around meatier topics. I was both fascinated and bored with how gently they acted toward each other. When the doorbell rang and the pizza arrived, I was thrilled for a change of topic.

The University of Washington Husky grinned on Leif's T-shirt while he piled his plate with five slices of everything pie.

"Head down into the family room. I'll be right behind you." Vivian pointed him off and turned her back, popping her enzyme pills and the handful of other things she had to take with dinner. Her piled plate oozed greasy cheese and hunks of spicy sausage.

"You eat as much as I do," Leif commented, stuffing half a slice into his mouth.

Nice manners, dude.

"Oh." Vivian set her plate down. "I'm supposed to eat like a bird, right?"

"Sh—t!" Leif's curse sounded more like "hit" and his horrified expression said it all.

She smiled and picked up a slice while he chewed and swallowed, trying to clear his mouth. She crammed a huge wad of pizza in her mouth.

He swallowed. "God, I'm stoked you eat. I didn't mean it bad."

Vivian nodded, trying to force cold soda into her mouth to cool the scalding sauce. There wasn't room. And there wasn't a way to appear polite and mannered. My mother would have gasped and died. I grinned.

"Girls who order salad and then spend the time staring at every bite I take like they want to eat me if I get in the way? No, thank you." Leif shook his head, then peered at Vivian's sweaty face. "Are you okay? That's a lot of hot pizza."

She nodded, managing not to choke and laugh at the same time.

"Slow down some." He handed her a napkin and another can of Mountain Dew.

They were just about finished when her mother strolled through the room. Maybe to chaperone, maybe because she really needed the roll of tape. "Vivian, when you're finished, you should give Leif a tour of the house. Show him what you painted on your walls."

"You've got paintings here too?"

"Her bedroom is very special." Her mother nodded and swept out of the room.

"So?" Leif asked.

"You really want a tour?"

He shrugged. "I like your art. Show me more."

"Okay." She stood and turned toward the door, missing the expression of pain that tightened Leif's muscles as he unfolded from the sofa. I saw it. Felt it. His knee and thigh screamed.

Vivian paused at her bedroom door. It was striped with a plaid of brights.

"Nice door. Very you." He nodded.

"Thanks." She pushed it open, glad she'd cleaned her room recently. She lunged forward to quickly kick a pair of dirty panties under the bed skirt.

"Wow." Leif turned in circles as if trying to take it all in.

I'd spent hours studying it before I could make sense of it all. Tiny squares of colors started in white and gradated out along the walls until it seemed as if we stood inside a rainbow.

"How long did this take?"

"I don't know. A long time?" she answered.

"Is every color ever made here?" He stepped closer to a wall and inspected the section of oranges, everything from peach to pumpkin.

"No, but most of the Pantones."

"What are Pantene colors?"

"Pantone." She smiled. "They're universal. So instead of saying tangerine and getting any orange, you can say 'Pantone 15-1247' and you get this tangerine color." She laid her finger on the square.

"That's kinda cool." Leif looked impressed. And then he pointed to another square. "What's that one?"

"Picante 19-1250."

"That?"

"Tigerlily 17-1456."

"Have you memorized all of them?"

"Most of them." She shrugged. "I've had a lot of time to waste."

"Seriously." He prowled around, looking at her photographs and trinkets.

She fidgeted, and rearranged, waiting for him to find something lacking or unacceptable.

Finally, he asked, "Where are you going?"

"Nowhere. What are you talking about?" Vivian frowned.

"Your luggage. It looks full." Leif walked toward the corner of her bedroom.

Vivian glanced at the weekender bag and small duffel. How much to share? How much to trust him? *Go for it. Tell him.* She paused before answering. "Those are my hospital bags."

"For what? Are you sick?" Leif's concern brought him steps closer, not farther away from her, and galvanized her to tell him the full truth. At least some of it.

"Before I had an organ transplant, I had to spend a lot of time in the hospital getting antibiotics, and being tested, and stuff."

"What kind of transplant?"

"Heart and lungs."

"Wow, but you're better now. You don't have to go back to the hospital."

"Not as much."

"How much time did you spend there?"

"If I was lucky? A couple of weeks every few months, or only a couple times a year."

Leif frowned. "That sucks, but I don't get it. If you're better, why didn't you unpack?"

Vivian shrugged. "A friend told me about keeping bags packed with everything I'd need all the time. She was older. I thought she knew everything. That way, my mom didn't have to go through my stuff and I didn't have to keep asking her to bring different things to me. I had it all in one place ready to go." Vivian's eyes welled with tears, and she sat down on her bed, hiding her face until she'd blinked them back.

"You look sad." Leif struggled not to offer too much comfort.

Vivian nodded. "I haven't thought about Tracy in a long time." She scooted over so he sat down too.

He nodded. "Did you have a fight or something?"

"A fight?"

"Girls fight a lot with their friends." He imparted this wisdom as if it was a secret.

Vivian started giggling.

"No?" Leif smiled sheepishly.

"Maybe on television, I guess. I don't fight with my friends, but then again . . ." She trailed off and sobered.

"Then what?"

She inhaled and exhaled her words. "Most of my friends are dead, or sick, like me."

"Oh." Leif froze.

Good, Vivian, scare the boy to death. Cue fast exit on three . . .

"I told you about my transplant? Well, it's because I have cystic fibrosis. It's not curable, and a lot of people who are born with it don't live a long a time. That's changing, though." She had no idea how to explain CF and the complexities of medical research in a few short sentences. She rushed her words together, feeling as though she was making things worse, with an explanation, and not better. "I mean, now the average is up to forty."

"Forty what? People?" Leif frowned.

"No, forty years. Most CFers don't live past the typical middle age."

"Wow. Oh. Wow." Leif seemed to gather himself. "But you've got new organs, right? That has to help."

"Well, yes and no. I still have CF, I just don't have lungs that are going to fail because of the CF."

"So you'll live a long time." He said this as though he some-how decreed it.

I saw Vivian struggle with being honest, but not giving false hope. She didn't want to scare him away, but she didn't know how not to.

He seemed to struggle with words. "You should be going on a trip. Where do you want to go?"

I wanted to kiss him for not running out the door. Who knew Leif had backbone?

"What?" Vivian leaned forward.

Leif changed the subject so fast I wasn't surprised that she had a hard time following either. "If you get half the time, you have to do twice the stuff." He shrugged. "Right?"

"Math isn't my strong suit." She gave him a small smile.

He grimaced. "Screw school. You need to spend all your time doing what you love. Painting. Pantone stuff. Whatever."

She shook her head. "Having CF doesn't give me license to goof off."

"So if you died tomorrow, you'd be happy you spent your last day in chemistry with Dr. Frances? That would make your life complete?" He snorted.

Vivian's mind's eye filled with pictures of beaches (Pantone 18-4525), evergreen mountains (Pantone 350), kissing (Pantone 199), opening her own studio (Pantone 214), seeing her work in the Met (Pantone 605). The shiny bright colors of a fantasy future swirled through her.

"Vivian? Viv?" Leif touched her.

She blinked.

"Where'd you go?"

"I was imagining a lifetime. And no, to answer your question,

I don't think I'd miss skipping class, but my parents feel like CF isn't an excuse to have fun all the time."

"Speaking of parents, I should probably head home and face the music."

"Sure."

"I'll call you?"

"Yeah, okay."

Vivian walked him out and laid her head against the front door.

"He's a nice boy. Were you studying?" her mother offered tentatively from the hall behind her.

"Yes, he is."

"Will he be back?"

"I don't know." Vivian wanted to be optimistic, but nothing in her life prepared her to be anything other than certain he wouldn't call.

CHAPTER TWELVE

Samuel wheeled his suitcase up the paved sidewalk toward the group of parents and boys gathered in camouflage and comic-book character accessories. His mother marched ahead like a tour guide, as if he might possibly miss the boy-scout-birthday extravaganza. One youngster already had orange Popsicle juice staining his T-shirt and layers of dirt streaked on his cargo shorts. Oh hell no. Samuel skidded to a stop. His was the kind of planted stance that started revolutions and government overthrows.

These kids aren't ten, they're maybe eight.

With an unexpected whoop of delight, Mrs. Wayland descended on Sam's mom. "Thank you so much for talking him into chaperoning. We couldn't do this without you." She spoke in that stage whisper adults thought out of range of anyone under eighteen. *Moron. Craptastic.*

Mrs. Sabir stared stalwartly at the trailhead and not at Samuel. So this wasn't just a setup; it was an ambush.

Mrs. Wayland stepped toward Sam, but kept her distance, as if she was afraid to touch him or contract a disease. *Mega-moron.* "Samuel. How are you feeling? Tip-top shape? Good, good. We've got fifteen young men for this adventure." She turned away. "Andy, stop eating the pinecones!" she shrieked. "Get that out of his hand."

Young men? Maybe in ten years. Right now they ate their boogers in public and peed wherever they pleased. These were not Sam's people; even I knew that.

Mrs. Wayland shoved her husband off his cell phone and whispered between clenched teeth, with angry points of a well-manicured claw.

I grimaced and cringed—at least, I wanted to. I think Samuel and I both felt sorry for her husband. *Speaking of bossy-pants.* She hurtled into a pileup of wrestling, or maybe fighting, boys. I had never quite understood the way boys pounded on their friends, and death hadn't provided any revelation.

Samuel's ma wouldn't meet his stare. He simply turned and started back toward the car. God himself wouldn't get Sam to stay there. *You go, Sammy!* I tried cheering him on, but no one noticed.

"Where are you going?" His ma sounded genuinely perplexed as she caught up with him, and moved in front to block his escape route.

He's mad.

After a heartbeat of swallowing anger, he said softly, "I hope you packed your hiking boots and favorite pillow."

She frowned with surprise. "I'm not staying. You are. You'll have fun."

"If you don't stay and police those boys, I think someone will get hurt, or be stranded where Air Rescue can't find them." Samuel's stony expression told me, and her, he was serious. Not that he would hurt a kid intentionally. *I think.*

"I—I—" she stuttered, her expression stunned and more than a little hurt.

"Ma, I am not a babysitter. I don't camp. I don't like the outdoors. I am sorry if I'm so disappointing to you, but I swear to you, if you leave me here with these delinquents, someone is going to get impaled on their weenie-roasting stick."

Oh boy.

"Yoo-hoo, Samuel, they're leaving." Mrs. Wayland pointed at the trail and the couple of dads who looked more like pack animals. There was nothing left of the boys but dust rolling down the trailhead.

Uh-oh.

Samuel and his mom stared at each other until she blinked. "I'm so sorry, dear, but I forgot that Samuel's medication prevents him from sleeping outdoors. He was so excited that he didn't want to remind me. Can you take him home on your way back? I'll stay instead."

"Oh." Mrs. Wayland seemed unsure what she'd walked into, or what the right answer was. She glanced back and forth as if at a Ping-Pong game.

Samuel merely handed his pillow to his mother. He kept his hand clenched around the handle of the wheeled suitcase; it was full of solar chargers and equipment. Nothing camping-related. Nothing that his mother knew how to use. *Not that he'd let her touch it.*

Under her breath, Mrs. Sabir promised, "We will talk about this when I get home."

Samuel nodded. Whatever.

Without a word, she blew up the trailhead at such a speed

onlookers assumed she was in a hurry to catch up. Samuel knew she was running from him. He sighed.

Mrs. Wayland reminded him to buckle up before she turned on the car. "Do you mind if we stop at the grocery store on the way back? I need to get more snacks and breakfast supplies for the campers."

"Fine." Samuel didn't care. His usual style of talk-to-anyone, anywhere, at-any-time flopped flat. He didn't want to talk to Mrs. Wayland, or the stock boy, or the cashier.

While Mrs. Wayland tried to chat him up one aisle and down the next, Samuel filled a basket with junk food. Chips. Microwave popcorn. A strawberry pie. Coke. A deli pizza loaded with preservatives and salt and meat by-products.

"Do I need to worry about a party at your mother's house while she's not home?" She eyed the contents of his basket with a worried frown.

"Of course not."

A party of one? Maybe.

She nodded but didn't look convinced.

Dropped at his house after what felt like hours, Samuel waved good-bye, thankful that she had no idea that his medication had nothing to do with his refusal to stay and "chaperone" the toddlers.

He tossed the pizza into the oven and switched on his monitors. "Who's out there?" Samuel pinged a couple of people, including Misty. He cracked open a can of bright red, totally artificial soda and gulped it.

S: wanna chat?

Yo, Sammy, artificial colors and sweeteners aren't exactly a rebel-lion. There's a reason "let them eat cake" wasn't cheered.

Sam sat back and waited to see who might respond. He belched. A new member ID on the MiracleMakers' roll caught his attention and he pinged that newbie too.

Or she. You have to quit assuming everyone is a guy.

Misty didn't respond, but PigskinPaint messaged back almost immediately.

```
PP: sure
    cool game
S: virgin?
PP: first time here
S: sure
```

Samuel grinned.

Definitely a guy. Why does everything have to do with sex?

```
PP: looking around
    how'd you come up with this?
```

The long answer was the hours, upon days, Samuel spent hooked up to dialysis. He blew through new games in one session or less, until all the zombies and coin collecting felt flat and obsolete. So he began writing code, learning how to animate and create a game that did more than blow shit up. MiracleMakers put the player in terrible situations—real life-wrecking situations like fires, floods, earthquakes, mass shootings. Players faced choices to rescue victims in high-adrenaline scenarios, or rebuild towns one brick at a time as deliberate, but slower, aid. Players built their miracle banks up and, thanks to Samuel's corporate sponsors, donated MM dollars to charities all over the world. It was playing with a purpose. He wished his mother understood.

```
S: seemed like a good idea
   we're all connected
PP: true
```

Samuel ate pizza and half a box of chocolate doughnuts while he worked on building level twelve. He wanted to go live with it next month. Recovering from surgery took longer than he'd thought. He hadn't been able to work much for months.

He checked messages.

Still no Misty.

Recovering from the kidneys and pancreas transplant wasn't as easy as it might sound. His body had to adapt to the new organs. He had to watch his food and beverage intake, his exertion levels, his stress. It took time to get it all functioning right. The healing exhausted him more than the disease ever had, and his mother's hovering made it all worse. She loved him. Maybe too much? He knew that too.

Almost as if she didn't want him to get completely better. As if his being sick gave her a purpose. Totally messed up.

Samuel wiped his hands on a dirty T-shirt because he'd forgotten to grab a napkin.

Ew.

He slid his chair around, switched between screens to update

The-Daily-Miracle. He liked his game almost as much as he liked his blog, but his blog was what got him out of bed in the morning.

He believed that people would rise to whatever expectation they were held to. That was his faith, that was what he loved about religion. Faith asked people to be better than themselves, bigger, more.

After deliberating, Samuel typed in his latest miracle, titling it: "Kid versus Gorilla—we all win." He wrote up the story as succinctly as he could; he wasn't a writer, didn't want to be. A kid fell into a gorilla pen at the Berlin Zoo and hit his head. The closest gorilla was the old silverback, notoriously bad tempered and territorial. With families of both species watching, the gorilla carefully picked up the child, cradled him in one arm, and carried the unconscious toddler to the door the keepers used. He gently deposited the child next to the door and backed away, as if he understood the keepers might be leery of opening the door. The child regained consciousness soon after the rescue. He sustained only a minor concussion and bruises, and he made a full recovery.

And thanks to technology, there were a dozen videos, from all angles, from witnesses who pulled out their devices to record the incident. Samuel wished that once, only once, someone would put down their camera phone and jump into action instead. No one leapt into the gorilla cage to save the kid. He shook his head. Could have been a whole other story.

PigskinPaint pinged again from the virtual game board. Samuel switched back and read the question.

```
PP: how'd you decide making video games was what
    you wanted to do?
```

```
S: deep question
PP: sorry man
     hoping for advice
S: give me a second to formulate
```

Samuel paused and downed another cold soda while deciding how to answer. People asked his advice all the time; thing was, most people assumed he was some video-game Yoda getting moldy in a tech fortress somewhere instead of a seventeen-year-old who'd spent most of his life hunting his own miracle. Not much life happened to him in hospitals and prayer circles. At least, not much he was willing to share with strangers.

```
S: i played video games
    a lot of games
    i beat them all
    i lost hours in that vortex
PP: i see that
S: got to the point when i surfaced i lost time
    and felt gross
    sounds idiotic to say but it was all pointless
PP: no i get it
     wasted time
```

Samuel took PigskinPaint's words to heart and opened up a little more.

```
S: i needed a reason to get up every day
    a purpose
```

PP: and you found it with the game?
S: some
    i like seeing where people spend their cash
    building a house isnt as sexy as taking out
    zombies
    but zombies dont feed people in Bangladesh
    either
    i also post a blog about daily miracles

Sam attached the link to the screen.

PP: will check it out
    thanks man preesh it
S: anytime

Misty pinged and Samuel checked the time. One a.m. What time zone was she in?
Pacific Standard.

M: hi Samuel?
    how r u?

CHAPTER THIRTEEN

S: hoping to find you here

Misty swallowed hard. The silence of books huddled around her like a blanket. Comforting instead of scared. Alone but not so lonely. Seconds ticked by. She didn't know what to say. She messed things up. Everything.

M: really?
   u look for me?
S: y
   2 much?

She exhaled a tiny feather of the guilt, the disbelief that ruffled her heart making it impossible to relax.

M: no
   glad to find u 2

There were so many words she wanted to type. So many things she wanted to know about him. So many things she wanted to tell him.

S: what time is it there?
M: idk
   L8

The blinker cursed at her. Waiting. Hoping. Judging.
Where do they go from here?

M: do u ever look at your hands and wonder why
   they're not busy?
S: i guess not
   why?

She didn't want to tell him that everyone around, always at
school or even during library hours, seemed to be texting, typing
with their fingers flying. Or playing games. Or something. Their
hands were occupied. Hers felt as though they simply hung at the
ends of her arms, vacant and irrelevant.

S: do u know origami?
M: is that paper folding?
   i wish i knew
S: y
   do you know sum people link a miracle healing
   to folding 1k paper cranes?
M: really?
S: many cases
   say it works
M: cranes?

Misty perked up. Healing?

S: sure
   1k paper cranes bring health and happiness
   either to the person who folds em
   or the person they are folded 4
M: sweet

The cursor seemed to stumble and tilt across the screen.

S: i can teach u
   i did a whole blog about it
   i got pretty good at it
M: 1k?
S: n
   i only folded 144

How hard can folding one thousand pieces of paper be?

M: does it have to be special paper?
S: n
   thats the cool part
   use anything—candy wrappers
   foil
   napkins
   just has to be square
M: can u tell me how?
S: ive got a camera on screen
   i can walk you through it live

Misty panicked. She started shaking. Trembling. She fisted
her hands and bit a knuckle.

She didn't want him to see her.

Calm down. You're going to rupture something important.

Misty forced herself to breathe past the fear. He couldn't see her unless she let him. She didn't have to. Gulping at the frenzy, she finally plunked back an answer one key at a time.

```
M: there's no camera on this comp
S: u sure?
   most have built in these days
M: really old
```

Misty's dry mouth mocked her, she tasted metal shavings each time she moved her tongue.

Focus on something else.

Come on, Samuel, distract her. I held my fingers crossed that he wouldn't push harder. She didn't want anyone to see her. I understood, except I wanted everyone to see me.

```
S: o
   ok
   will go step by step when youre ready
   do u hve paper?
   u need a square
   start big
M: why?
S: easier big
   to learn
```

Misty pulled out an assignment sheet from her backpack and folded it until she could rip the crease straight off. Samuel walked her through folding a crane, waiting each step for her to type *next*.

Misty's first crane looked more like roadkill than intricate art-work, and it broke at least six laws of biology and physics. *No way will that fly.* She started the next bird but paused to ask Samuel a question.

```
M: if u weren't talking to me what would u be
   doing?
S: research
M: on what?
S: its not very happy
```

Misty understood unhappy better than happy.

```
M: that's ok
   tell me?
S: im researching accidents and obituaries of
   people in the western US
```

Way to sound like a serial killer, Sammy! I wanted to roll my eyes at his honesty. *Now she'll never reach out again.*

```
M: oh
S: im not crazy
   or sick
   or anything

S: say something
```

S: anything

Misty chewed on her bottom lip.

M: why?
S: thnx
   becuz im trying to find a particular dead
   person

Misty swallowed, wondering if she was too sick to know when she should be afraid. But she wasn't fearful, simply curious as to what seemed the safest possible question.

M: why?
S: for answers
   idk
   complicated
M: isn't everything?
S: someday i will tell you
   ok?
M: sure
   someday you can tell me
   right
S: what do u mean?
M: never mind
S: dont do that
   hate when girls do that
M: do what?

```
S: say something important
   and then act like it wasnt
M: oh
   i just don't think you'll tell me
   that's all
   and I'm sleepy
S: u r forgiven
M: i'm sleepy
   i need to go
S: ok
   night
```

Misty yawned as if she hadn't slept for days, maybe months. But her stomach rumbled so she navigated her way to the front desk looking for snacks, or candy, or something. She found a stash of old Halloween candy. Tootsie Rolls. Individually wrapped. Half a bag, tossed behind hand sanitizer and a box of tissues. More riffling produced a can of diet shake.

The irony wasn't lost on me.

She didn't have her complete dose of meds with her, but she swallowed the yellows and grays and a couple of the whites. There were too many to name. She'd take the rest before school in the morning. She'd just go back to the apartment early. That was only a few hours away. No way that would hurt anything.

Are you sure?

The morning janitorial crew came in weekdays at six. She'd sneak out of the library then.

Leif turned up the volume on Kenny Tislane's newest country album. He'd listened to it enough that he sang along without even realizing it.

I sang along and I hated country music. *Why does he have to love country?*

Leif trolled the Internet looking for "how to play guitar" videos and "how to play Kenny Tislane" blogs the way I suspected he used to troll for porn. I wanted to grab the guitar and hit him over the head with it.

I knew nothing about the instrument, or what it took to play it. Well, I used to know nothing, now I knew a lot. *Thanks, Leif.*

Like chords. His chords sucked. I didn't know if they were flat, or sharp, or just plain wrong, but they hurt my ears and sounded nothing like Kenny.

Like strumming versus plucking versus whatever he was doing. *At least he's graduated from holding the guitar like a football.*

His brow furrowed and dug deeper into his sight line with concentration. The last note played in the playlist and he sighed. "No freaking closer." Frustration dripped out, and off, his fingers.

He mimicked his dad's favorite phrase. "Closer just is 'See a Loser.'" His dad was almost as full of crap as his mom. It's no wonder this kid walked around without deigning to speak to mere peasants. Everything was a competition, and if he wasn't on top, he was on the bottom.

Leif dug his cell phone out of his pocket. His parents took the landline phone out of his bedroom, but forgot to confiscate his cell. *Shows how often he disobeys them, doesn't it?*

"Art and Soul, this is Cassidy."

Leif winced. He wanted Vivian to answer. "Uh, hey."

"Hi. Can I help you?"

"Is Vivian working? It's Leif."

"Oh, Leif." She drew out his name as if there was a full stadium of meaning in there. I wanted to giggle.

"Yeah, so is she there?"

"No, she's not working, but here's her cell." Cassidy rattled off numbers and he grabbed a marker, wrote the digits on his arm. "Got it?"

"Yeah, thanks."

"She's in the middle of a portrait, so she'll probably be in later tonight." Cassidy's voice sounded full of smiles and double entendre.

"Great. Thanks." Hanging up, Leif stared at the phone. Should he call her?

He dialed the first five when he heard, "Hey, son, dinner's ready."

He tucked the phone into his desk drawer and headed down to face the winner's circle, aka the dinner table.

CHAPTER FOURTEEN

Misty hesitated outside the cracked concrete steps of the apartment building. Every time she returned, part of her hoped magic had turned it into a home, but it was as desolate and depressing as always. Most of the inhabitants were either still asleep because they worked late or were already at work and not back to sleep during the sun's reign.

Uh-oh.

Her grandmother was up and doing her creepy usual. Even from the outside hallway, Misty heard the chants and prayers and muttering. Her feet cramped, her toes tangled in protest. Immediately, the feeling of loathing crawled up her spine and tickled the backs of her eyes until her head throbbed. The old lady would glare and spit and point. It was their routine.

Misty hesitated. Her pills were inside the apartment. She had to replenish the Ziploc bags she carried with her.

You need your pills. You have to go inside.

She waited. Debated.

Her hand clenched the key to the deadbolt.

Someone's footsteps skittered down the stairs above her. A big rat or a small dog?

I wanted to squeal and hop around, but Misty didn't even react to the sounds. Her gaze glued to the door and what she knew was on the other side.

She turned around. Away from the door, from the apartment, from the pills.

Wait. No, you have to take your pills.

Misty!

Misty!

I shouted and waved and couldn't make her even hesitate a second.

She never glanced back. I couldn't shake the sick feeling that this was a horrible decision.

Family dinners with Leif's parents seemed a legitimate part of his grounding punishment. They gathered at one end of the glass and chrome dining-room table that comfortably sat the starting lineup for the Packers. The dishes were glass with silver edges and matched the tumblers and silverware perfectly. His parents even wiped their mouths with perfectly pressed squares of white linen threaded with silver accents. Together, it felt cold, calculated, chosen solely for appearances.

"What is it you're listening to up there?" his dad asked with a jab of his fork.

Leif tucked his napkin into his lap. "Music."

"Not twang country? Crossover rock and roll?"

"What's wrong with country music?" Leif asked. It wasn't classical for his brainwave development. Or rock like his dad preferred, those urban notes that stayed on the surface and didn't slither in the mud of humanity.

His dad jabbed again, shaking his head. "Those aren't our people."

Anger bubbled up but Leif stuffed it deeper. He felt as though in letting one beat of emotion go he'd lose control of all of them. His dad's view of the world seemed to narrow the older Leif got. Maybe Leif just widened his eyes and his dad didn't change.

After setting the filled plates down before them, his mom launched into the conversation Leif dreaded most. "We need to talk about the upcoming fall schedule and your training regimen."

That's months away. I cringed for him, but he tried not to react outwardly. Inside, he boiled and raged and screamed for a break.

Leif shrugged noncommittally, keeping his eyes on the plate of perfectly baked salmon fillet, a bare chicken breast, blanched kale, and broccoli trees. *Yummy.* If he was lucky, he'd get a protein shake for dessert. The menu for winners in this family required lots of vegetables and mostly protein; carbs were complex and came with a fiber minimum per serving. His tongue begged for the everything pizza at Vivian's.

His dad continued where his mom had left off. "I've been fielding calls from scouts all spring, son. They're waiting on offers until they see if you can play up to your potential."

It's as if they're afraid to speak about his injury directly.

"Because of my leg?" Tension vibrated from each obvious word. He'd been hoping they'd lay off. Give up. Let him breathe. Leif set his fork down. His appetite was gone. Until then, they'd ignored the new loud country music in his room, the secondhand guitar he'd dragged home, the crayons and paints that littered his desk and bedroom floor.

"All athletes have to lose occasionally. It's how the great ones evolve," Mom stated.

He didn't lose, he was injured. I half expected her to add, "Confucius say." *Condescending much?*

Leif lifted his gaze, hardened and flinty, as if daring her to continue. I shuddered.

The pent-up frustration inched closer to his surface. "And what, I'm a great one?"

"In this family you are. Certainly not a loser." His dad's voice rose with the elevating tension.

"What if I can't?" Leif asked.

His mom gasped. "We don't use the word *can't*, Leif. You know that."

He shoved his plate away. "What if my leg won't work the way it used to? Would it be the end of the world?"

She paled, her fork clattering to the table. "Give up football? You're kidding."

"Now isn't the time to joke around, son."

I felt him trying to push back, to hold his ground, without losing his temper. "It's my life." He wanted them to hear him, listen to him.

"And you don't want to play professional football anymore? Is that it? Wanna sell me ice in winter, dumbass?" His dad knocked over his chair when he stood.

He's trying to appear bigger, more intimidating. Stop bullying your son!

"John!" Leif's mom sounded appalled, but ruined it by continuing. "Leif, we are athletes. That is who we are. You can't waste your talent. We won't let you."

"Let me?" Leif pushed back from the table and thrust away from them. I prayed his knee wouldn't buckle and suck the drama out of it.

His dad isn't taller anymore—does he know?

"Leif!" Dad yelled.

"Son!" Mom added at top volume.

"Let me?" he repeated, shaking. He'd never disobeyed them. Ever. Their expressions said it all. They didn't know how to deal. Their perfect son stomped from the room and slammed the front door. He broke into a jog that quickly turned into a full-out sprint. He ignored the shooting pain, the crackling of scar tissue, the pop of a joint still healing.

I wish I could stay behind and listen to his parents. But then again, they probably didn't speak for hours. The shock was that epic.

The knock on the glass door of Art and Soul jerked Vivian out of her thoughts, but she ignored whoever was out there. Closed meant closed. She'd been staring at the eyes for the last hour. Eyes made up of tiny butterflies of cream (Pantone 9180) and songbirds in chocolate (Pantone 732). But they weren't quite right. The richness of the brown mellowed the cream, but didn't pop. They seemed sad. She frowned when she heard the door rattle again.

Then pounding started.

Someone knew she was inside.

She put down her paint and tubes and rolled her head around her shoulders. It was late. After dinner and the store was closed on Sunday nights. No missed calls on her phone and no messages.

She crept toward the front of the store, wondering if one of the street's nighttime residents was looking for a place to sleep. It wouldn't be the first time. When she saw Leif's hair, the top of his head haloed under the entrance's light, she slowed her step. Relief surged, followed by anger, glazed with another emotion she couldn't name, but made her giddy.

"He hasn't called," she whispered to herself, hoping to hang on to a little of the mad. She hadn't heard from him since pizza at her house. She thought . . . she thought he'd decided he didn't want to be her friend. It wouldn't be the first time her reality wasn't the pleasant picture most envisioned. He wouldn't be the first to run in the opposite direction.

Leif's hair was wet, not from sweat, but from the steady fall of rain outside. When had it started to rain? His expression broke her heart and made her fingers fumble with the keys. She hurried to unlock the door and step back. But she didn't know what to say.

He hesitated, dripping at the threshold.

"Coffee?" she asked.

He nodded. A shiver racked his shoulders.

Broad, muscular, sexy shoulders. I wasn't the only one thinking objectified thoughts.

Leif followed Vivian back into the darkened workroom; spotlights from single flood bulbs illuminated her easel and area, but left the rest of the studio plunged into shadow. The light washed out the color and softened the edges of the room. It made it easier for her to focus on the canvas.

"Sugar? Milk?" she asked, heading toward the break room.

Leif's arms were crossed and she saw the little muscle on his jaw clench and unclench as if out of habit. "Lots of each."

"Don't look, okay?" Vivian pointed to her easel when she reached the doorway. She didn't want to leave him alone if he'd peek.

"Is it me?" Leif grinned.

"No."

"Fine." Leif shrugged, as if it wasn't a difficult request to accommodate.

Curiosity is not his vice. Personally, I'd have snuck over and taken a gander at it, especially since she told him it was a secret. He stayed exactly where she left him. His entire brain was focused on the future, and choosing to goof off like guys at school. About becoming the very thing his parents feared most. A loser.

Vivian's heart sped up, my heart thumped, and she quickly inhaled a breath for calm before she stepped back into the studio. I'd have done the same thing.

"It's late for a workout, isn't it?" Vivian handed him a mug, and sipped her hot chocolate.

"Skipping family dinner," he replied.

"You do that a lot?"

He squinted. "What?"

"Skip out on things?"

Leif chuckled, almost spilling his drink with surprise.

It's a fair question.

"What'd I say?" Vivian asked.

Leif huffed disbelief. "I don't skip out on anything. I am the guy who understands obligation and commitment." He lowered his gaze. "I even went to extra physical therapy and doctors to make my parents happy. The sports medicine doc didn't know why we were there. So, no, I don't quit anything. This is only the second time I've walked out."

She hemmed, thinking, then asked, "The first was the award thing?"

"Yeah."

Silence of palest blue (Pantone 9044) with edges of soft pink (Pantone 677) drifted between them.

Leif opened and closed his mouth several times. She waited for him to find the words, sensing that he needed to share, but in his own time. "Three hours after I woke up in the hospital, my dad told me that the lap record was twenty-three."

"Laps around what? The hospital floor?" she asked.

"Yep. He expected me to double that."

"How'd he even know there was a record?"

"He probably asked. 'There are records all around, son. We only have to know them to break them.'" Leif deepened his voice and added a layer of bitter to his tone.

Curious, Vivian asked, "So did you? Break the record?"

"Of course." Leif answered as if it was a given.

"He sounds harsh."

"Maybe. I don't know. I didn't used to think so."

"Why'd you leave dinner tonight?" Vivian's thoughts wandered to Leif's eye color, wondering if the color came in a tube, or if she'd have to custom mix it.

"Promise you won't laugh?" He finished his coffee in a gulp.

"Promise." Vivian said the word with the fullest possible intent behind each letter. She promised with all of her.

"I've been playing with the guitar. Writing songs."

"Really? That's awesome." And so not what she expected to hear.

You don't want to hear.

"You think?"

She nodded vigorously. "Way hard to write a good song."

"That's just it. I don't think they're any good." Lamenting, he shook his head.

"And you know how?"

He's a genius.

"I don't." Leif laughed, his glance darting toward her easel. "Did you always know you wanted to paint? I mean, once you started—is it what you were meant to do?"

"I think I've always seen the world in colors."

"Like those Pantimi—"

"Pantone." She smiled.

"Sorry, it doesn't stick."

"That's okay. I don't know the first thing about breaking records. I'm more a middle-of-the-pack girl."

"That's not true." The intensity of Leif's gaze made Vivian turn twelve shades of red on the inside. So many hues, she couldn't even begin to name them.

He continued. "You paint people, right? But they're different than usual. What do you call it?"

"I paint the parts of people no one sees. All the pieces, all the miracles that go into making them who they are."

"You sound like this guy I know. Everything is a miracle."

"It's true, though. Most people take time for granted."

Leif agreed. "That's what I'm trying to avoid."

"What did you say to your parents when you walked out?"

He ignored her question and countered with his own. "Where do you see yourself in five years? College? Painting? What?"

Where did Vivian see herself? The only place Vivian knew for sure she'd be was in the cemetery, and even then she didn't know if that was tomorrow, or next week, or ten years from now. "I don't know."

She really doesn't.

"You must have an idea."

"I don't. I try not to think too far ahead." She shrugged, returning his gesture.

He sighed. "And I can't stop."

"What do you mean?"

"My whole life has been a schedule. My parents decided I played football in the fall, then ran track in the spring to keep in shape for football. That I will win the Heisman and be drafted in the first round."

"What about concussions and stuff? Don't you have to worry about that now?"

"According to my dad, bell ringing is part of the game."

"You believe that?"

"No, but they do, and that's all that matters."

"I don't get it. Why can't you stop?" The idea of planning anything, let alone a life like Leif's, was a foreign concept to Vivian.

"If I don't work out hard this summer, I probably won't get my starting spot back. If I don't get a starting spot, the scouts won't come, which means I'll have to go to whatever college wants me, which means that affects my Heisman hopes, and the draft and what team I get or if I even get drafted, and—"

"Stop! I get it. I get it." Vivian set her cocoa down. "You really think about all that?"

"How can you not? With painting or whatever?"

Why didn't she? The answers were easy. "What's the point? God laughs at our plans. Why not take everything one day at a time?"

Leif frowned. "How do you not set goals?"

"I have goals." *Did she?* Vivian paused. Didn't she?

"Like what?" he pressed.

"What everybody wants—a family, a house, a job I like."

Sure, those sound good. Pull something else generic out of your happy rainbow ass, please.

"Is that what everyone wants? 'Cause this last year none of those things were on my list of goals," Leif replied.

Vivian didn't know. Most days she thought about the next meal, the next dose of pills, the next physical-therapy torture session. Not amorphous future wishes. No one got guarantees; why be disappointed in something she couldn't control? "What do you want? Really? Don't you want to play football?"

"It's what I'm known for. It's what my parents think I'll do."

What was she known for? For coughing in the middle of videos so loudly the teachers paused until she left the room. For missing events because she was hospitalized for treatments, or blockages, or infections. For being the weird short girl who looked as though she belonged in the elementary school no matter what grade she was in. "Right, but what do *you* want?"

"That's what I'm trying to figure out. See what else might be out there. What do you really want?"

"I told you. I take life one day at a time."

"That's good. But then what?"

"What do you mean?" Frustration sizzled and popped (Pantone 166).

Slow down, Leif, you're pushing her too hard. She's going to snap.

"What career do you want? Where are you going? Do you want to live here or move somewhere else? What's on your bucket list?" Leif stood and paced. He rattled off questions in a rapid-fire, no-nonsense way that made Vivian cringe.

She stared back at him, unable to even begin to answer.

He broke it down into single bites. "Do you want to go to college?"

"Sure." Her tone suggested he change the subject.

"Where?"

"Uh—" Vivian shifted in her seat. She wanted him to stop. Needed him to stop.

He plowed on, oblivious to her agitation. "Get married? Have kids?"

"Sure. Maybe." Her expression dimmed; she, too, stood and crossed the room away from him. She gave him her back and waited for the stinging knife of reality to ease.

"What'd I say? Don't all girls want kids?" Leif asked with utter sincerity.

Seriously? Is he a Neanderthal? Me have womb, must have baby.

"Um, no, they don't." Vivian wasn't about to tell him that her CF and antirejection meds made being a mom something she really couldn't think about. It went into the column of things she shouldn't think about. Didn't think about. Not yet. Maybe not ever.

"Oh, sorry." He stopped.

"It's okay. I should get back to work. I need to go home soon."
Vivian randomly picked up paint and held it up for him to see,
like a prop.

No, it's not okay.

His expression tortured, he knew he'd wrecked their fragile
trust, hurt her, and made her angry. But he had no idea how to
begin fixing it.

Boys.

"Really. Can you go?" she insisted.

"I'll see you later?" he asked.

"Sure," she answered, but her breath held until the front door
smacked shut behind him. He didn't mean to be insensitive. She
knew.

I knew she wouldn't sleep tonight. Not with thoughts of Leif
and her impossible future racing in her mind.

CHAPTER FIFTEEN

"**Vivian, baby, we need to talk,**" her mom called out as Vivian came down the stairs the next morning.

For a heartbeat, she wondered if they'd received a phone call from the doctor.

Which one? Why?

Both of her parents sat in the living room wearing the same weary expression (Pantone 19-6110), but their gazes seemed tinged with anger.

Disappointment? Frustration?

Vivian braced herself, and automatically I did too. There was a universal gleam in parental stares of negativity.

"Your teacher called."

Vivian nodded. Which one?

Any of them. All of them.

"You're failing history," her mom offered.

And soon Spanish, and math, and chemistry. Should have studied for that test instead of painting. Instead of watching classic ESPN to try to learn football terminology. Instead of daydreaming about Leif even though you're mad at him.

Her dad reprimanded her gently. "We've always been so proud

of you. You've kept up your studies and your grades. Even in, and out of, the hospital. All these years you've done so well."

"What's going on?" her mom added, as if there must be an explanation, a reasonable one, like a misunderstanding, or a prank phone call.

They spoke to her as if she might break every time they discussed anything serious. As if they were afraid she'd die with their last interaction one of anger. They tiptoed. Her parents meant well. My mother would have lectured me on how it looked to fail. Appearances were not at the top of Vivian's family motto. I envied her that. But only that. They watched her as if *their* lives depended on it, not hers.

She cleared her throat. "Nothing's going on."

"Something's changed." Her dad shook his head.

"Is it that boy?" her mom asked.

"No." Vivian didn't sit down. "I've been busy."

"Too busy for school?"

I saw them share a glance and I wondered if they'd discussed a strategy before we got there. They seemed more united and more willing to upset Vivian than I'd ever witnessed.

"Then we need to clear your calendar."

"Mom." Vivian shook her head.

"If you can't work at the store, and paint, and do your schoolwork, then we have a problem." Her mom's words and expression pushed with the strength of steel (Pantone 18-4005 TCX).

"You need to paint less, or quit your job," her dad added.

"School is not the part of your commitments that should lapse."

For Vivian, the idea of not being around her paints, her colors, or the studio filled her with a searing heartbreak of swirled emotions. Part fiery pain (Pantone 1797) and part suffocating blackness (Pantone 19-4305).

"My painting pays the bills," Vivian reminded them, with a hint of her own anger. Her medical bills were astonishing, but ever since her career took off, the money from the paintings she sold paid for more than only her medical expenses. They couldn't mean give up painting—not really.

I think they might.

"And is your college fund," her mother reminded her.

"But we've discussed this, you don't have to pay—" Clearly uncomfortable discussing money, her dad backpedaled.

"Yes, I do." Vivian trembled. She refused to listen to her parents pace or sit at the dining room table with piles of bills and a calculator late into the night like they had when she was little. Not ever again.

"We would figure it out," her mom stated.

"How?" She turned toward her mom. "And I don't need a college fund."

They gaped and spoke over each other. "Why not?" and "You don't want to go?"

She gave them a bland stare. "I don't know."

"You don't have to work for minimum wage."

"I love working at Art and Soul."

"Well, you can't love everything." Her mother's exasperation gained momentum.

"I don't love school!" Vivian shouted.

I blanched at her tone, but for the first time heard self-confidence in her voice. *This is new.* Maybe the last time the kids made fun of her ate at her.

"Vivian!" her dad shouted.

Her mom stood. "You don't have to love school. It's necessary."

"Why is it necessary?" Vivian enunciated each word, a hammer to a nail.

"Because it is."

"That's a good reason." Vivian rolled her eyes.

"Don't do that, young lady."

"You need to graduate so you can go to college."

"And get a good job."

They were so agitated, none of them noticed they shouted, hoarse and raspy.

These people don't yell.

Vivian's brow filled with thunderclouds. "I have a job. I am a painter, an artist. Why do I need college?"

"It's important."

"For what? Why?" Vivian threw up her hands.

"Are you simply trying to be difficult?"

"I've told you how much I hate going to school."

"But you don't cough anymore."

"No one seems to know that but me," Vivian answered.

"Do you want me to talk to the principal again? He could make an announcement," her mom offered, softened with the reminder that Vivian was an outcast at school.

"No. Don't you dare!"

"I'm just trying to help."

Her dad stayed focused on his main point. "You're going to college."

"I am? I don't think so."

"Over my dead body," he growled.

"Over yours? How about mine?" she roared, then slapped a hand over her mouth as if to capture the words, but they were free.

"Vivian!"

Her parents whitened and grayed (Pantone 9320 and 656), the air sucked from their lungs, the heat extinguished completely. They sat heavily, silent, as if trying to comprehend how she could say that.

She means it.

Vivian licked her lips and blinked. "Well, that's what we're pretending, isn't it? That I have four years to study stuff I don't care about before I die? If I'm lucky, I won't die in the middle of my freshman year and leave you without a college-graduate daughter." The snide in her tone was coated with grief and sadness that hurt so much I wanted to escape it by any means possible. *She doesn't look ahead because it hurts too much.*

"You don't know what you're saying."

"You are not going to die."

"Yes, I am. Sooner than most people."

"With that attitude, young lady, of course you will. You have to be positive. Think optimistically."

"What attitude? Reality? I shouldn't have to go to school."

"Be realistic, then. You're at school about twelve days a year. It can't possibly be that bad." Her dad loved math and logic puzzles.

"Don't exaggerate, it's not helping," her mom chastised Dad.

"Not that bad?" Vivian agonized. "They're worried about making the basketball team, or if some butt-scratching boy like, *likes* them. They don't get it. None of them understand."

"You don't give your compatriots enough credit."

"I don't know what you think happens, but they make fun of me for being short, or coughing, or being sick, or all the side effects of the drugs that make me break out and grow hair like a damned Chia Pet."

"Vivian!"

"School is non-negotiable," her dad repeated.

"The CF doesn't change the rules for you."

But it should.

"I know. You've said that my whole life." Deflated, she gave up.

"And look what a life you have." Her mother began sniffling. "You have life unexpected."

Her dad closed his eyes. "And we got the biggest gift of extra time. More time with our precious girl."

Her mom cried. "We got a second chance with you."

"Parents shouldn't have to bury their children," her dad agreed, wiping his face on his sleeve.

Vivian couldn't bear the raw grief that flowed over her parents' faces.

"I know." She gave in. Gave up. Just gave. I didn't blame her for caving; it was as if they didn't hear her. Couldn't hear her. Their expectations that she beat the CF cast her in a warrior's role she didn't want.

"You have to fight harder, Vivian," her mother reprimanded.

With his arms around his sobbing wife, Vivian's dad dipped his head toward the doorway. "School Monday. No arguments."

"Yes, sir." She scuttled out of the room, but collapsed at the top of the stairs. With her arms tight around her knees, Vivian laid her head against the banister and listened. She'd learned long ago eavesdropping was the only way she discovered the truth about her health.

"She can't die." Her mom broke the words into puffing breaths.

"I know."

"We can't let her give up."

"I know."

"She doesn't understand how hard we've fought."

"I know."

"She has to want to live. I think she's losing her will to live. How can she throw away her future like that? Just when she has new lungs?"

They don't understand.

Tears of grave dirt (Pantone 17-1436) filled Vivian's eyes. It wasn't that she wanted to die young. She couldn't avoid it. Her oldest friend from the CF floor had been twenty-eight when he'd gotten new lungs. Then he'd died eighteen months after the transplant. She hadn't even gotten to say good-bye.

CHAPTER SIXTEEN

Parents shouldn't have to bury their children.

No, they shouldn't. Children should grow up, marry, have babies, retire, and then the parents, after they are grandparents or great-grandparents, should drift off into sleep one night and never wake up.

At least, that's what I used to think. Why did I assume that was inevitable? Like that was the way the world worked for everyone?

I never went to a funeral before I died.

Vivian was at fifteen and counting.

Samuel went to six.

Leif, at least, buried three of his four grandparents.

I didn't even go to my own funeral. I didn't know why I couldn't go, but maybe because I was connected to the pieces of me-still-living and not the parts that were buried that day. I didn't even know where my body was buried. *Why do I care?*

I'm not alive.

But I'm not dead.

I tried smacking light switches and making Samuel's monitors go fuzzy. I tried to invade the sleeping dreams of them all, but aside from knowing the dreams as they experienced them, I influenced nothing. Not a moment. *None of these people know me.*

Misty walked by my memorial case on the few days she went to school, but she never lingered.

Vivian rushed by it once.

Leif was never scheduled in that part of the school.

Samuel's cousin Rebecca, my locker neighbor, left a postcard of an angel tucked into the corner of it. Not because she knew Sam had my pieces, but because she was sad she hadn't gotten a chance to know me. Would I have noticed her death? Would I have gone to her funeral? Did any of my classmates attend mine?

CHAPTER SEVENTEEN

Samuel narrowed his search down to Oregon and Washington. Idaho was a wash. Sixty obits, ten car accidents, but only two organ donors. A little more digging told him neither was the right age, or organs, for his donor.

"I'm having lunch with Father Kelly; then I'll pick up dinner groceries." Mrs. Sabir stood in the doorway of his bedroom. The strain between them since the camping trip was fierce and palpable.

He barely glanced up from the screen. He was so close.

She frowned at the additional strings and clippings hanging from the walls, the ceiling. "Samuel, aren't you getting a little carri—"

Carried away? You think? Thank you for noticing.

"Hey, Mom, can you get more sauerkraut?" He interrupted her and ignored her question.

"Should I call Dr. Myers?" She crept closer and touched his forehead as if feeling for fever.

"Why?" He jerked away from her hand.

"You've eaten three jars this week. Maybe it's a side effect of the medications?"

"I doubt it." But he stopped and wondered.

Good question. Why are you eating tons of pickled cabbage when you don't have to?

"Then why are you eating so much of it?" she queried.

"I don't know. It tastes good." Samuel shrugged and turned back to his search engine. He entered the keywords *teenager, died, sauerkraut* and hit Enter.

His mother never gave up on anything. She wouldn't start with this. "I could never get you to eat sauerkraut when you were little."

"Maybe—" Samuel waited to see if he got any hits with his search.

"What?"

"Maybe my donor liked, um, sauerkraut."

Uh, no. I liked Sour Patch Kids. Sour jelly beans. Not sour cabbage, or sour socks, the way it smells.

She shook her head, obstinate and positive he was wrong. "I gave you those packets on cell memory. There is no evidence that people who think they like something new because of their transplant are right. It's a silly theory."

"Maybe." Samuel shrugged. He knew it wasn't worth arguing with her.

"I'm calling the doctor."

"Fine. But pick some up too, okay?" Samuel tried changing keywords, and order, and every combination he could think of. No hits. He made a note.

Seriously? Who would put sauerkraut in their kid's obituary? Even if they loved it. My mother would say I drank sparkling formula and used caviar to teethe on. Something that sounded extraordinary. Not sauerkraut.

Leif's world shrank to the basics under extreme parental scrutiny. School, home, covert phone calls to Vivian, online chats with MiracleMan Sam. His life was so different grounded. It was as if they feared he'd go from liking country music to being a felon in one fell swoop. But Leif didn't miss practice. Didn't miss working out. School was his only official social venue and even with that it lacked appeal.

"Hey, Leif."

"Hi." Leif bit his tongue rather than tell her she was in his way. She stood there expectantly and he realized he was supposed to know her name. Karin? Kara? Kasey?

Karly! Even I know she's the senior most likely to be Playmate of the Year.

He gave up and inwardly sighed. "What's up?"

"A bunch of us were talking and your name came up and we wanted to know . . . Do you have a date for prom?" She tossed her head and a whiff of vanilla body lotion tickled his nose. He didn't feel anything but annoyance.

Huh.

"Don't girls ever do anything singular?" he muttered under his breath. "It's always 'we.' Like a herd."

True, unless we are outcasts, and then we beg for herds.

"No, I don't." Leif hadn't even realized it was prom season. Last year, as a sophomore, he'd gone with Ashley before she graduated. A group of the team went together, partied into dawn, slept the day after. Nothing R-rated happened, but it was more because he didn't find drunk girls sexy than because she was unwilling. He'd gone because it was expected. He didn't want to go this year. He was tired of expected.

Hmm . . .

"Oh, great. That's great. So—" She lit up like he'd handed her a puppy.

Oops. Craptastic. Even I saw this train raging toward the wreck. He stopped her before she embarrassed herself. "I'm not going. I already have plans."

"Oh, oh." It seemed as though she couldn't quite wrap her head around the idea of scheduling anything up against prom, let alone picking that other thing.

Even over you.

"See ya." Leif stepped around her and didn't look back. If he hadn't been so focused on getting away, he would have realized I wasn't the only one paying close attention to the conversation.

Vivian watched Leif talk to the modelesque beauty. She ducked into an alcove instead of walking by them. She studied Karly. Wondered if the head toss was a gesture normal girls were born with. Karly got flirting and instead, Vivian got CF.

I felt Vivian's envy of Karly's typical beauty. What color would Vivian say jealousy was? Green was given, but what universal Pantone?

Behind you, dammit, behind you!

Vivian was so engrossed in spying, she was quickly cornered by a couple of tall, gangly bullies who routinely sought her out for sport jabs.

"Hey, phlegm-face. Haven't heard you cough much today." A couple of the jerks pretended to hack up innards in coughing fits so bad they should break ribs.

The alcove offered no escape route, but Vivian shimmied toward the side and leaned around the corner with her back to lockers. With the acumen of a veteran, she tried to ignore their taunts. And on the outside it appeared she did quite well. *Inside, not so much.*

I wanted to shout at them, they were so common. There was nothing special about picking on the tiny girl who coughed a lot. *Nothing.*

Rage (Pantone 485) and fear (Pantone 5405) and weariness (Pantone 15-0942) battled inside Vivian until she choked on emotion, breathing around tangible colors. This was why she hated school. This was what her parents didn't understand. This was the uselessness incarnate of why she didn't belong here.

At least be creative in your targets, you craptastic Neanderthals.

"Come on, we're just kidding. Don't cry."

"Yeah, don't cry. Your snot will drown us all." They chuckled and high-fived.

Inside Vivian's head, I heard our middle-school guidance counselor repeat that bullies must feel powerless in their own lives to get a rush out of this behavior. *I wish we believed him.*

A teacher poked her head out of her classroom with a frown—maybe it was the volume of their taunts, or maybe a special teacher sense finally kicked in—but it was enough to give Vivian room to squeeze past and hurry away.

Vivian refused to allow them to witness her tears. She'd long ago given up crying because people were mean. If she cried every time someone made fun of her she'd never stop.

She simply wished—

Her phone beeped. Incoming message.

Vivian read the words without really seeing them. As if the message downloaded the situation, the emotions, in one fell swoop. "Sally in ICU. Time is short. She wants to see you."

Another friend dying.

Someone give her a break. Please?

Vivian stashed her books in her locker and left her homework in there too. This was why she didn't bother to worry about school any more. What was the point?

What is the point? I echoed her thoughts in agreement.

She headed toward the exit and passed Leif, who was bent over a drinking fountain.

"Hi, Leif," she said, slowing her step.

He didn't look up. Didn't stop drinking.

The jerks followed her and began coughing again.

Vivian didn't want Leif to see them, or hear them, or ask her about them. He never looked at her as though she was sick. She didn't want that to change. So she rushed on, wondering if he'd noticed her and ignored her, or if he really hadn't heard her say hello.

She headed toward Memorial Hospital. Sally was barely thirteen. Why can't she get lungs and a heart? Why had Vivian instead?

Why had I lost mine?

CHAPTER EIGHTEEN

Misty snuck a wad of papers from the recycle bin, under the copy machines, on the library's first floor. The bright papers and crazy prints were a total score, even if wonky and wacky on the misprinted pages because the copier was drunk, or high, making concert flyers. White copy paper made boringly white cranes.

She weaved through tables of college kids studying for finals and a couple of senior citizens playing chess, to the nook she considered her real home.

Everything appeared just as she'd left it. The computer wasn't even turned on.

While the screen spun and booted, Misty sharpened a pencil and logged the latest set of medical bills into a makeshift ledger of lined paper. Notices about overdue, and unpaid, and lots of red stamps made her shrink deeper and deeper inside herself. She'd pay them. *How?* She wasn't trying to get away with anything. But if they'd asked her? She would have picked an easy death last October over this constant fight to just not be miserable.

She means it; she'd rather be dead than misery's burden to the world.

My heart ached. She logged on to MiracleMakers' message center and waited.

Nothing but the blinking cursor, and her friend Sam, seemed easy. Nothing was. Misty typed again.

M: u wanna chat?

After several weeks of messages, she'd picked up Sam's favorite phrase. When he didn't immediately respond, she assumed him busy. He was always there. Always available to chat with her. She depended on that. On him.

He's getting sausage and sauerkraut, but he'll be right back.

I worried that Misty depended on this cyber connection to get her through each day. How fast had this relationship become her whole world?

It's amazing how time loses meaning when there is only one good thing in a sea of pain.

While she waited, Misty began making the rectangles into squares of all sizes. Folded creases ripped quietly against the corner of the desk.

S: whats up Foggy Morning?

Misty's delight when Sam's message popped up was effervescent, as if she'd swallowed happy and it poured out each pore.

M: happy to see you here
S: o crse
   im always here 4 u

With each typed line, Misty folded a crease, or two, of her origami cranes. So that every few minutes her flock hatched another bird.

Sweat went from damp to dripping along her brow and caused a shiver of goose bumps to line her arms.

There's something wrong with her.

I knew she worked up to asking Samuel her question of the day. She'd been thinking about it constantly.

```
M: do u believe in God?
S: do u?
M: no
S: why?
M: i don't think he can exist in a world like
   this.
S: u mean wars
   & famine
   & bigotry?
```

No. Misty meant families like hers, working until they died, trying to find purchase on the ledge. Her obligations to them. To the world. To this miracle she had been given and would like to give back. God couldn't be present in any of that.

I haven't seen him either. Just saying.

```
M: that 2
   if u believe in God
   then what r u?
```

```
S: hmm
   do i have 2 be something
   2 believe?
M: y
S: im a little bit of this
   and a little of that
M: u don't have to tell me
```

The cursor added layers of hurt and rejection to the screen without Misty saying anything about how she felt them.

```
S: n
   im not dodging
   i like the stories
   all of them
   Moses & Muhammad werent that far apart
   i even like the passion of zealots whose faith
   is so strong that intellect has no place in
   their narrative
```

Huh? Sometimes Sam made me dumb by default.

Puzzled, Misty frowned. What was he talking about? She thought of all the check boxes on the forms she had to fill out. Wasn't it a simple question? Christian? Jewish? Muslim? Other?

```
M: english?
S: the people who see life so simply that their
   worldview is black & white
```

```
right & wrong
u or me
they see no negotiating or compromise
```

Her thoughts immediately went to her grandmother's shrine of gold paint and beads and burning spit.

```
M: u like that?
S: i didnt say i could be that
   but
   i envy it
   how easy life must be for those
   who see it so clearly
   life is only complicated when u
   can see angles & degrees
```

Vivian would add color to that list.
Misty's eyes watered, but she refused to call them tears.

```
S: u there?
M: y
   what else do u think about God?
```

Thrilled that he was answering rather than asking her why she cared, Misty fell a little more in love with Sam.

She doesn't even know he's a teenager, too. He could be elderly, and in prison, and she'd be thrilled.

```
S: i like the serenity i see in buddhism
   they dont get all riled up
```

```
           not like christians
           or muslims
           or jews
M:  they don't?
S:  have u ever heard of extremist buddhists?
    zen terrorism?
```

Misty giggled.

```
M:  that's terrible
S:  try it—
    whats a zen terrorist do?
M:  they hit people over the head with bells
S:  passable
    but u can do better
M:  they 'om' until people go nuts?
S:  better
M:  they insist everyone wear those robes
    and half of the redneck world kills themselves
    instead of wearing a dress?
S:  thats awesome
    i can see the confederate flag
    draped over willie tom's gut in an elegant
    sarong
```

Misty laughed, but stifled herself, fearful of calling attention to her hiding place in the stacks.

```
S:  u dont believe?
    in anything?
```

```
M: no
   i can't see a purpose
S: thats sad
   i wish
```

Don't, Sam. Don't say it.

Sam let the cursor blink and Misty waited, her fingers frozen on the printout of a tie-dye album cover, soon to be the neck of a crane. I hoped he'd follow his intuition or listen to me for once and change the subject.

She finally typed to him.

```
M: u wish what?
S: will u describe yourself to me?
```

Panic ripped through Misty's gut.

```
M: BRB
```

She stumbled down the stairs, leaving her bags behind her, and headed for the handicapped bathroom tucked near the children's section.

She locked the door and flipped on the light.

Bent over the sink, Misty stared in the mirror and saw a monster superimposed over the real her. The her she used to be. Five feet and delicate, waist-length black hair that was so shiny the light hit it and zapped all color away, leaving a mirrorlike reflection. Her eyes were bright with humor. Her lips a perfect pink bow. Her skin clear and clean.

But the monster outside was hideous. Puffy and bloated. Her face round, her fingers stubby and meaty. Her skin was mottled with spots, pigment rashes, and dry, flaky patches that were astonishingly slick with oil. Her hair seemed permanently dirty, slick at the roots but dry and brittle at the ends. It frizzed up as if she was standing near too much static electricity. Her eyes were beady, and sunken, behind the bags and doughy lids. She alternated between too cold and too hot. Sweat pitted out every shirt. So no matter the temperature, she wore a thick, heavy fleece to cover herself. She was sure she reeked of rot.

She saw nothing in the mirror of her true self. Should she describe her real self or the new monster to Sam? He never needed to know the truth.

Gathering her hair into a knot, she tucked it up under the hood of her sweatshirt. She wet her face, then filled her palms with mounds of foaming antibacterial hand soap. Scrubbing until the pale skin was red and the inflamed places angry. With her nails, she scratched off the whiteheads of pimples and the crusty scabs of healing ones, the flakes of dead cells collected under her nails, and still she knew the oil lurked. She hit the water faucet continually, keeping it roaring and steamy, as hot as it could possibly get in those fifteen-second intervals.

Stop, Misty. Stop hurting yourself.

I tried to stop her. Hug her. Soothe her. I wanted to rub lotion on her skin and salve on her broken heart. The self-loathing radiated out until the bathroom filled and I felt like we drowned in it, like treading water in the middle of the ocean without reprieve. It was killing us.

The handle jiggled and someone knocked. *Finally.* Someone noticed her suffering. At least, they needed the toilet.

Misty wadded up the recycled fibers of paper towels and scrubbed at her face. Taking away the water, the soap, and trying to diminish the horror of what she saw.

Describe herself?

Misty no longer knew herself.

Returning to the computer, determined to change the subject, she hoped he never asked again.

CHAPTER NINETEEN

Leif felt antsy and awkward. He'd negotiated a cease-fire with his parents. If he ran five miles a day, they'd let him out of the house to socialize. He lied about the running. They'd freaked when he stopped using the home gym, when his mother no longer did six loads of sweaty workout wear a week.

Vivian greeted him at Art & Soul and he got to work. He wasn't about to upset her again. He wished he knew what he'd said.

"Can I see what you're working on?" he asked Vivian.

"Take off your pants," she answered without looking up.

He must have heard wrong. "What?"

"You heard me," she said, smiling in her voice and on her face.

He liked seeing her bright smile. It lit her from the inside out and reminded him of summer vacations. He wanted her to do it more often. She'd been full of frowns and degrees of sadness since he got there, and he didn't think it was because of him. He wished she'd tell him what she thought so hard about. If he thought she'd laugh, he would strip in a heartbeat. His hands stayed planted firmly in his pockets. "But—"

She set down her chisel and microscopic brush. "It's not that easy to get naked in front of a stranger, is it?"

"You're not a stranger." Leif showed her his fingers and made a move toward his waistband. He called her bluff.

The blush that heated her neck to forehead flew up at the speed of light. She coughed as if clearing her throat of a tickle, but really she floundered for a response.

"So, you're not really asking . . ." He stopped fingering the button.

And this sounds like a dare. . . .

Vivian crossed her arms and I knew she was about to return his bravado. "Only if you want to see my work in progress." An excited kind of fear sent shock waves through their bodies. I wasn't sure who was more amped, but neither wanted to back down first.

I'm about to see more than I want to. . . .

His heart thumping with nerves and more than a little desire, Leif touched his zipper, then laughed in surrender. "I'm not ready to, you know, show you the goods. Not even for a peek at the painting."

Smooth.

Vivian giggled. It wasn't an embarrassed laugh as much as an appreciation of both his push, and his retreat. He understood her. Got her sense of humor. Saw the world at least a little from where she stood in it.

Vivian poured her heart into all of her portraits. I knew who she wanted to be painting, but she was a long way from being finished. Like anything done with this much heart, it took hours of work, days of early drafts that were messy and convoluted and verbose.

No one got to see the portraits until she was certain the meaning was clear and easy to read. Not even Leif. As tempted as she was to let him peek. Stripping and streaking might very well come easier than opening an unfinished piece to his critique.

Leif wandered, as much because he wanted to diffuse the crackling tension as because he found that without the strenuous workouts, he overflowed with movement. "What's that one on top?" He pointed at a stack of canvasses leaning against the studio wall.

"Me."

Leif made a show of looking down and checking his pants.

"What are you doing?" Vivian asked.

"Why aren't they finished? Why's it sitting here for people like me, with pants on, to see?"

"Very funny."

"No. Seriously. What's the problem?" He studied her and the canvas.

Vivian walked over and fell into the swirl of paints and colors. The vortex of her organ failure and subsequent transplant rushed at her as if an opponent in a boxing ring hit the ropes and came swinging back. "I was working on it when . . ." She stopped, the words knocked out of her throat by the emotion of memory.

Leif pressed. Like a typical guy, he knew she was upset, but not how much. "When what?"

"Right before the transplant."

"But you're better," Leif stated, though I wasn't sure he truly understood that Vivian would never get better, not completely. "What haven't you finished?"

Give the boy a gold star for asking the obvious.

Because she didn't know if the transplant changed her. If she was part of someone else. Vivian specialized in portraits made up of tiny nuggets of pictograms. What was the sum of her parts? Had that changed? Had her donor changed her, or was it just the experience of lying on the edge of death that made her feel this way?

It's not me.

Vivian weighed her options. Did she share the truth? Or did she make up a stupid excuse about not liking it?

Tell him the truth. He can handle it.

How much fact could he handle? He knew about the CF and the transplant. So far, he hadn't run away. But he had to be on the edge of bailing. No one stayed around by choice. People liked easy answers, easy lives, stories that resolved and ended. Vivian's story was an endless loop of a broken body that never resolved. Not in this life anyway.

"What are you afraid of?" Leif asked, as if reading her mind.

She pondered. "I don't know." She couldn't give him that much of herself. She wasn't even sure she understood it all. Her greatest fear was that if she finished the painting, there would be nothing left for her to do (Pantone 383).

Ah, that's a scary feeling. She seemed surprised by the feeling; I didn't know it was there either.

Leif licked his lips. She noticed. He did it every time he was choosing his words carefully. As if easing the right words out from a tight space.

Vivian stepped away. "Sorry, I can't—"

Talking about her death was a sure way to chase him off. And maybe that would be easier than looking forward to seeing him and hoping he'd be different. A melancholy blue settled like a rock in her stomach (Pantone 535).

"It's okay. I, um . . . never mind." Leif didn't understand what he'd said that was so terrible.

I wanted him to push Vivian. *Prod her. Make her face this.*

He turned to leave. I tried to block the door, but all I managed to do was knock a few books and notecards over. *Oh my god! How'd I do that?* I tried to move more books, but nothing happened.

Leif immediately dropped to his knees to pick them up, and Vivian hurried over. She was desperate to fix the mess she had made by not answering him. She had to say the right thing (Pantone 7548) to help him understand and see. Before he left and never spoke to her again.

"I should have died," she blurted, kneeling down next to him.

"When? Why?"

"My heart and lungs were infected, scarred from the CF. I kept coughing up blood and they couldn't get it to stop."

Leif sat back until his butt hit the floor. This cocoon of truth under the tabletops and around the chair legs felt precarious and fragile.

Vivian eased to a sitting position as well. "My friend Sally just died."

"Did she have the same thing?"

"CF." Vivian nodded. "But they didn't find lungs in time. I was lucky."

"Do you feel lucky?" Leif's expression was mystified and his heart beat so loudly I wondered how she didn't hear it.

"No one's asked me that."

"So?"

"No. Yes." Vivian shook her head. "I should have died, but someone gifted me another chance with their organs."

"Gifted?"

"I don't know. I've been trying to think of the right word to use. Donation seems like something you do with your old jeans, or spare change, or soup cans, right?"

Leif nodded. "True."

"And what better gift could there be, really?" Vivian cringed. "It's life. There's nothing to compare to that."

"True."

They lapsed into silence there on the floor of the instruction manual aisle. I moved away, feeling like I was intruding, though I still felt and heard and saw everything.

Squared, in this case.

Leif ended the silence, demanding gently, "Tell me about your friend who died."

"Which one?"

"There's more than one?"

Vivian nodded. "This will be my sixteenth funeral."

"Wow." He rocked back. "All kids?"

She thought for a moment and then answered, "The eldest was twenty-eight; the youngest, six."

"They all had CF?"

"No, you meet lots of different kinds of broken bodies when you spend a lot of time in the hospital. The peds ward is full of cancers and birth defects and terrible accidents."

"What kind of accidents?" And I knew Leif's mind had turned to the incident on the football field, while I was thrown back into thinking about the car accident.

"Car accidents, near drownings, fires. I don't know, stuff that they talk about on the late-night news. Will you tell me what happened?" She gestured to his leg.

"To me?"

"Yeah, you limp. Sometimes it looks worse than others."

"You can see that?"

"Yeah." Vivian blushed, as if he'd caught her doing something illegal (Pantone 17-1564).

"Most people don't notice. But then, you're not most people, are you?" Leif said this last bit in a whisper almost to himself.

"Please?"

Yes, Leif, tell her.

CHAPTER TWENTY

We all turned to thinking about that night. I still smelled Mother's perfume and that reeking alcohol. Leif felt the sweat on his back and grass beneath his feet, smelled the crisp fall air and the stench of ancient sweat-stained uniforms. Heartbeats and play counts filled the room around us. Vivian waited, innately understanding that what she'd asked was difficult to answer.

Leif blew out a breath. "Is it weird that I heard it before I felt it? Like it happened outside of me, and inside, at the same time?"

Vivian shook her head. "Sometimes I think I hear my heart stutter like it's sending out an SOS to its original person."

"Really?" He frowned, automatically rubbing a hand over his thigh, his knee, his shin.

"When it happened, did you hear a pop?" Vivian pressed. "Guys in the hospital who blew out their knees always talked about a pop."

"Some, but it's not like I was just running and it blew." Leif shook his head. "My leg vibrated and crushed in, bone on bone, like that sound when you smash a hard-boiled egg on the counter."

Ew.

Vivian managed not to flinch. "When did the pain hit?"

"Not until I tried to jump back up and fell down. I saw everyone's face and knew it was bad. I guess I passed out at some point."

Vivian's fingertips touched his wrist. A moment of understanding.

"Have you seen the video uploads?" Leif asked.

She grimaced. "There are videos? Why would anyone want to watch you, anyone, get hurt like that?"

"I don't know." He shook his head. "I lived it. I don't need to watch it like a movie. But my dad thought it was motivation. He played them over and over again on his phone while I crutched laps around the hospital floor."

"Oh. Your dad sounds—"

"Like a winner, right? He was a professional quarterback. My mom was a gold-medal Olympian in three Summer Games. They run marathons for fun." He deepened his voice as if announcing a starting lineup. "We are winners. Champion Leolins."

"Wow." Vivian understood the pressure; it had to be similar to her parents' need for her to live. Win. Live. Same dif.

"Watching those videos made me want to puke. The audio was the worst part. Will you come with me? I want to show you something."

"Now?"

He staggered to his feet. "Yeah, right now."

Vivian wasn't sure what she expected, but the neutral beige (Pantone 4685) of the exterior and the interior decorations of Leif's house wasn't it. She thought perhaps there might be Olympic gold medals hanging from the ceiling and a scoreboard above the dining room table. It could have appeared in any decorator magazine and offended no one.

They snuck down the lower hall. I recognized the squeak of the exercise bike and click of the weight machines: his parents were working out again. *They're obsessed.*

"Gym," he whispered, pointing upstairs.

He held her hand and ushered her into his bedroom.

Her curiosity overcame any shyness, but I noticed the stiffness in Leif's shoulders, as if waiting for her to find fault.

For a moment, after he clicked on the overhead light, Vivian's brain jumbled. How in the world did he expect her to react? She dropped her bag off her shoulder. "Um . . ."

Don't scream and run away, for starters?

Leif sighed. "It's hideous, isn't it?"

"Do you get lonely?" Vivian asked, gazing at all the life-size wall decals and cardboard cutouts of people. Most of them in some sort of athletic uniform.

"What?" Leif asked.

"All the people." She waved her hands around. "It's kinda crowded in here, like a full stadium."

"Oh damn." Leif glanced around. "They're not mine. My parents think that I'll be inspired to be like Mike, or Derek, or Lance."

"Or Tom, Dick, and Harry?" Vivian was shorter than all of them, and in the corners they were three-deep, like a true crowd.

"Yeah, it got worse when I got hurt. Used to be I'd just get one for Christmas and birthdays."

"Did you ask for them? Like one year I wanted My Little Ponies."

"No, I asked for things like CDs or video games."

"I don't see any gaming stuff?"

"I never got what I asked for." Leif's shoulders relaxed.

Vivian shook her head. "How do you sleep with all of them watching you?"

Leif shrugged.

He hasn't thought about it, girlie.

"Do you change in the bathroom?" Vivian pushed.

I giggled.

His eyes widened. "There are more in there."

"No!"

Leif leaned down toward her. If it were a movie he'd kiss her, but Vivian knew he couldn't possibly see her that way. She stepped back, ostensibly to check the bathroom.

The shower curtain was a photograph of football players in helmets and uniforms.

"That's the offensive line of the Raiders." He laid his hands on her shoulders.

He's making moves, don't run away!

"I thought you were kidding." Vivian felt a shivery blossom of potential that scared her (Pantone 7493). Returning to the bedroom, she grabbed her bag and dug through it, finally pulling out a set of paint pens.

Leif crossed his arms but his smile was amused. "What are you doing?"

"Closing his eyes." Vivian drew a blindfold over LeBron James's fierce gaze. "He's watching."

Leif held out his hand.

"You want me to stop?" Vivian deflated and started to hand over her pen. "Sorry—"

"No, give me one too." Leif painted a pair of silver sunglasses over Tedy Bruschi's eyes. Then added a mustache.

"I like that."

"He needs a nose ring." Leif nodded at Lance and smiled when Vivian dotted a bit of gold over one nostril.

Joy (Pantone 12-0727), comfort (Pantone 17-4021), and passion (Pantone 18-2326) arched between them like sparks of current.

I sat on the bed and watched them mutilate the army of athletes on cardboard, plastic, poster, and vinyl cling.

Colors that coordinated, or clashed, with team colors became facial hair, sunglasses, Zorro masks, bandanas, leis, and hats. Within an hour, they'd turned the mass of top athletes, winners by the Leolin standard, from a weird, staring chess set to a traveling concert crowd.

Vivian dumped her bag out, looking for paper scraps to re-mascot the uniforms.

"Do you have the entire art supply store in there?" Leif leaned down. "What are we looking for?"

He reached forward, accidentally drawing a line across her hand.

She gasped. "You did that on purpose."

"No, I didn't."

Mischief bubbled up in Vivian and she giggled through the stern face. She slashed red across his cheekbone. "Oops."

Leif's eye bugged; he grabbed a second pen while Vivian scrambled backward. "You don't know what you started."

"I didn't start it, you did!" she squealed, trying to put Larry Bird between them.

Leif caught and held Vivian, but he let her slip away and hide behind RG3 as if the quarterback came with an Invisibility Cloak.

They stumbled up and over the bed, tagging each other with colors until the laughter and the paint blended seamlessly.

My lungs filled and expanded to an insane capacity. As if all the tributaries and branches of my oxygen trees felt the breeze of this exertion for the first time.

"Mercy!" Vivian cried, collapsing into a baseball-shaped bean bag.

With a badly hidden wince, Leif threw himself down next to her. They panted and chuckled. Just the sides of their forearms touched, but it was enough to zing them both with skin-on-skin sensations.

"Oh no." Vivian gasped.

"What?" Leif shifted to look at her, his hand easily gliding over her waist until his arm draped across her.

She pretended the cuddling was ordinary when it felt anything but. "Don't tell your parents."

"Don't tell them what?"

"They missed a spot. Your ceiling is bare." She pointed up.

Leif followed her finger. "Oh, damn. You're right, but then I really *would* have people staring at me while I slept."

You have me.

Vivian asked quietly, "God does, doesn't he?"

"Yeah, but his face isn't painted on the ceiling." Leif smiled.

"We could paint it." She turned her head slightly toward him.

And I haven't seen God around here. Or anywhere.

"I'd rather not. It would make it harder to do what I want to do if he was watching." He leaned up onto his hand and stared down at her.

"What do you want to do?" Vivian's words whispered across his cheek, but she froze as if afraid to break the moment.

Vivian didn't break eye contact. My heart thumped. We were going to kiss. For the first time. Love with its vitality and promise bloomed deep within Vivian (Pantone 19-2025).

Leif licked his lips. "I read this thing about CF. Are you really extra salty?"

She nodded, holding her breath.

Leif dipped his head and laid his lips featherlight against hers.

The barest hint of dawn awakening colored that kiss (Pantone 11-4804).

CHAPTER TWENTY-ONE

Misty logged back in.

```
M: sorry
   line @ the bathroom
S: u dont have a computer at home?
M: no
S: i thought maybe id offended u
M: no
   why?
S: i dont care what u look like
   just wanted to picture u when we talk
M: u might be a perv
S: true
M: u don't deny?
S: im not
   but cant prove it.
M: ;)
S: make u a deal?
   tell me who u wish u looked like
   i wish i was like Krispin Reed.
```

Misty quick searched for images of Krispin. The actor was ripped, tall, tan, and Hollywood elite. There were images of him with a girl, Calliope Dane. She was exotic, petite, and perky. Everything Misty knew she wasn't anymore.

M: then i'm Calliope.

S: wow
   what a coincidence

M: tell me something people don't know about u

S: like i have a foot fetish?

M: i don't even know what that means.

S: jk

M: 4 real

S: im closing in on finding my organ donor

M: 4 real?

S: yep
   i have kidneys
   & a pancreas I wasnt born with

M: me 2!

S: truth?

M: not kidneys but a liver
   i think i went to school with the girl

S: thats heavy
   why?

M: they told my parents that the liver came from
   a teenager in perfect health
   and i was very lucky
   a local girl died the same night

S: and u think u went to school with her?

M: yeah if it's her

```
it's not like we were best friends
i mean she probably wishes someone else got
her liver
like the homecoming queen
```

Like a Skirt? Not likely, thanks.

```
S: i hope that in death we move beyond petty
   differences
   no popularity contests
M: r u sure u r only 17?
S: y
   why?
M: sometimes u sound like a x btwn a fortune
   cookie
   Yoda
   and an old man
```

Samuel stuttered and couldn't make his fingers move. I chuckled. My thoughts exactly.

```
M: sam?
M: i'm sorry.
M: i didn't mean to insult u
M: i just
   it's weird
   u know how to talk about this stuff
   and never have met u
M: I guess I'm—
```

```
S: dont be sorry
   u r right
   sometimes i feel like a fortune cookie
   sometimes i look like Yoda
   & sometimes i definitely feel like an old man
   but yeah
   my birth certificate attests to the fact
   im only 17
```

They traded questions and revelations, quotes, and favorite things. It was easy to open up logged in. There was safety. Anonymity. A quick escape route if things got too personal.

```
S: whats one thing u loved to do
   when u were little?
M: swing at recess
```

Sam looked out his window and spied his neighbors' tire swing in a big old tree.

```
S: can u take your comp outside?
   r there swings nearby?
```

Misty didn't glance around, didn't move. She was sure there were plenty of swings mentioned in the tomes around her. Photographs and people, real and imagined, who were sitting on swings right this minute.

```
M: sure
```

Sam grabbed his tablet and wandered outside in the dark. A flashlight app showed light on tree roots and discarded toys. He sat, digging into the earth with his toes and heels.

S: what do u see?

Misty closed her eyes.

M: stars
   moon
S: my moon is waxing
M: then so is mine
   right?
S: any shooting stars to wish on?
M: maybe a couple
   out there somewhere
S: what would u wish?
M: u first
S: id like to find out who my donor was
   who he was
   what he did
   if he left family behind
   why he donated his organs

She. She. She.

M: that's more than 1 wish
S: laffing
   true
M: i wish I could go back in time

```
S: to medieval England
   or dinosaurs
   or something?
```

No, like to the night they saved her life. She wishes they hadn't. I don't know how to feel about that at all.

```
M: do u ever think about what would happen
   if u hadn't had a transplant?
S: id be on dialysis until they couldnt do that
   anymore
   & then
   die
S: misty?
S: what about u?
M: i wasn't sick
   or anything
   not like bad enough to see a doctor
```

She didn't mention the weight loss, the pain, the headaches, and bloating. She didn't tell him that she would have never gone to the hospital except for George's phone call to 911.

```
S: what happened?
M: my grandmother says i got infested
   with the demon
S: she sounds
   ummm
   nice
M: she hates me
```

```
S: u cant be too fond of her either
M: not really
   at least she's honest
   more than i think my parents r
```

Misty thought perhaps her parents hated her too. Life was hard enough before that night, before the doctors and the surgery and the bills.

```
S: r u serious?
M: maybe
S: u had acute liver failure?
M: something like that
S: u know u didnt do anything
   to get liver failure
   right?
```

Go on, Sam. She doesn't know any such thing. Tell her she doesn't deserve this.

```
M: maybe
S: im serious
   ive spent a ton of my life in hospitals
   & around sick kids
   liver failure can happen
   without anyone doing anything bad
M: sure
S: i dont believe u
   i think u actually believe u couldve avoided
   it
```

I watched her struggle how to answer. How did she explain that this was all her fault?

You can't. Because it's not.

She typed, deleted, typed again and watched the cursor blink at her.

M: maybe
S: u r kidding
   did u drink scotch instead of breast-feed
   or something?
M: no
S: misty u cant control your organs
   i know lots of people who think positive
   thinking
   or negative thinking can affect our lives
   but this kind of thing isnt about thoughts
   parts stop working
   they can be defective
   do u blame yourself if the television
   wont turn on?
M: but
   maybe
   if
S: NO
   absolutely NOT
   why havent your parents told u this?
   what about your doctor?
   your social worker?
   have you told anyone u feel responsible?

Misty withered. The doctors spent five minutes with her, less if they figured out she was uninsured. The social worker called in the beginning, but who was she anyway? And Misty's parents? Her parents didn't talk, they yelled, and were always about blame.

```
S: misty
   talk to me
   im sorry
   i probably came on too strong
   listen to me
   plz?
```

Sam took a deep breath and I nudged him mentally to continue. Misty couldn't hear me. No matter how loudly I screamed. Maybe she'd hear Samuel if he said the words.

```
S: there r stupid people
   who end up with liver disease
   becuz they drank too much
   but kids
   we get other things that we cant control
   at all
   ever
M: maybe it is a demon
S: please tell me u r
M: KIDDING
M: ☺
S: Ok
   good
```

```
M: I have to go
   they're shutting down
S: Promise me youll think about what i said
M: sure
   night Samuel
   aka Krispin
S: night Foggy Bottoms
```

Misty hated her family's rented apartment, but she needed food and to change her clothes. She worried a librarian might start to notice if she left clean laundry and a pillow near her cubbyhole. She wanted someone, anyone, to notice her, like at the hospital. But if they did, then she'd lose her sanctuary.

There wasn't a good way to be at home with her family. Misty missed the hospital. Not the being sick part. The having people care about whether she was in pain, or feeling nauseous, or sleeping part.

She watched a new mom finish making copies of a college textbook while burping a sleeping baby. A young man came over, gently took the baby, and kissed the mother on the lips with an expression full of love.

The hospital was full of families who helped each other, touched, and hugged. The parents she watched sleeping in chairs, in the tiny spaces between walls and beds just to be close, in case the child had a nightmare in the middle of the night. Misty slept alone with the monsters for company instead.

The families who showed up every day with a new treat, with balloons and stuffed animals, and lots of handmade cards from classmates, or siblings. Misty's parents didn't spend nights with her because they worked multiple shifts. The only card she got was from her brother. She wasn't imagining it. They glared instead of hugged. They blamed her for getting sick. They blamed him for calling the hospital. Grandmother blamed them all for bringing her to this godless place. No wonder the demons found a home.

George rolled over when she crept in. "Where have you been?"

"Studying."

"I saved you chicken. It's behind the moldy cheese."

"Thanks." Her stomach turned. "I ate. You take it for lunch tomorrow."

"Are you sure?"

"Yeah."

He nodded, then dropped his voice another notch toward silence. "The school called twice and left messages. I deleted them."

"Did they hear?"

He shrugged. "I don't know."

Grandmother's snores whistled, paused, hiccupped, then began again. Misty rubbed her legs, it felt as though a million ants trekked in circles up and down her limbs.

George whispered, "Don't you have to see the doctor soon for checkups?"

Misty turned away from her brother, relieved that the darkness hid her. He saw more than anyone else, and she didn't want him to see the lie in her face. "Last week." She'd canceled. She couldn't afford the five minutes because she knew they'd want tests and more tests and new drugs. Enough already.

You didn't go because you don't feel good and you're afraid.

"Oh, how'd it go? They have to do a biopsy?" George sat up

and scooted over so she had room next to him on the pallet. *He's too little to have to understand words like* biopsy.

"Fine. Good. No, next time," Misty mumbled, and felt his expectation like the weight of a million rotting livers suffocating her. Why did he care so much? Why did he ask?

"You went, right?"

"Of course I went." Anger flared and made her voice vibrate.

"Sorry!" He held his hands out in surrender, grabbed the blanket, and turned over.

The only questions her parents asked were about the bills. The pills. Money.

"I'm an ass. I'm sorry." Misty touched his back.

"Are you okay?"

"I promise. I'll be fine. Just a big test coming up."

"Okay. I have a piano recital on Thursday after school. Can you come hear me?"

"Sure. Of course." If something happened to her, who would go hear George play his music?

CHAPTER TWENTY-TWO

Grief colored the entire world like an overlay of drudge. Vivian stared at the mound of dirt set off in the distance that no one was supposed to notice. The small, strikingly purple casket (Pantone 18-3025) disappeared into the earth as people moved away. She'd watched Sally's parents sob against each other, and the surviving siblings huddle together.

I gazed around. *Is this where my body is too? Will we walk by my gravestone? Do I have one?*

Leif didn't let go of Vivian's hand, and I wanted someone to hold mine too. Vivian's mother never came to funerals with her. It was too hard.

As if it weren't a big deal, Leif skipped school and drove them to the church and then to the cemetery. For Vivian it felt like a huge deal that he came with her (Pantone 3278).

But Vivian was out of tears. When she died, what would mark her time on earth? A hole in the ground? A stone with her name on it? Anything permanent?

Your paintings will outlive us all.

I can't say it ever occurred to me to wonder. *What's my legacy?*

I never even thought about the leaving, so thinking about what might linger wasn't part of the equation. But I got it. I understood why she was fixated.

Leif spoke quietly. "I liked what the minister said about death being a heavenly birthday."

Vivian's mind filled with a lively party scene. A whole world of purple and pink, balloons, cake, and presents. Sally was more vibrant and beautiful and wholly healthy, enjoying the reunion with friends.

Is that what heaven is? A party? Then why am I not there?

Vivian tipped her head to look up at Leif. "Do you believe in heaven?"

"I'd like to."

"Me too." Vivian had buried her friends for as far back as she remembered. First they were the older kids who knew the ins and the outs of the hospital. Who brought luggage to turn their rooms at the hospital into a home away from home. Who told her how to get through a test, or which nurse might sneak in ice cream after visiting hours, and who to avoid letting put IVs in at all costs. Sally was too young to know any of those friends.

But then, they were kids Vivian's own age, maybe younger, but frequent fliers she met for the blood tests, and the PFTS, and the biopsies. Or met in the hospital during antibiotic treatments, the friends she Skyped with and texted, when they were too sick to hang out. Friends who also spent a great deal of time thinking about heaven's existence.

And then somehow Vivian became the elder, the oldest kid in the ward who knew all the tricks and all the nurses. That was when she'd met Sally.

"I'm going to die," Vivian declared.

"We all are." Leif shrugged her off.

"Yeah, but you'll be a grandfather first."

Leif tried to make her smile. "You'll be a cougar."

"No. I will die young too." The sincerity in Vivian's voice sliced at Leif.

"You can't know that. What are you talking about? You're so wrong." Leif couldn't keep his voice low. His reaction carried on the wind over the mounds, between the crosses.

Vivian snorted. "I'm wrong?"

"Yeah, you are, I Googled CF. There's an eighty-two-year-old."

"So?"

"So that's old. Freakishly old."

"It's not that old for a normal person."

Leif huffed and licked his lips. "You're more normal than most people I know."

She refused to lighten up. "Don't be funny. I'm serious. CF colors everything."

"What color?"

"The color of snot when you have a bad cold. Pantone 15-0543."

He grimaced. "Yuck, I can actually picture that. But why that color?"

"My entire childhood was spent dealing with the stuff of slime monsters. Trying to get it out of my lungs, hawking up loogies and hanging upside down to drip it out." She paused. "People don't live more than five or six years with new lungs."

"So? You'll be the first lung transplant to live sixty years more.

You'll set a new standard." Leif nodded his head as if decreeing the future.

Vivian knew this was unlikely; she wanted to hope, but it felt so impossible. She knelt and tossed in a handful of dirt onto the shiny purple of Sally's casket. The sound of the particles hitting the lid was so final. So permanent. "Maybe I got some old person's lungs. You think to Google that?"

"You didn't."

"No, probably not."

Leif grabbed her hand and wound his fingers through hers, fiercely, as if trying to hang on to her forever.

They climbed back into the car and Leif drove toward Vivian's. The radio played a mix of pop tunes and make-out music. I usually avoided cars, but I sensed a serious conversation on the horizon. Probably because I knew what they both thought in each moment. *Will come in handy when I figure out how to work it.*

"Do you think about your donor?" Leif finally broke the silence.

"All the time."

"Do you want to know who he, or she, was?"

"I can write them a letter and if the family wants to meet me too, then we can, eventually. There are rules."

"Okay, so write them a letter."

"I think I might already know."

I held very still while Leif pulled into the driveway and shut off the ignition.

"What? How?" Leif nudged her chin up until they made eye contact.

"There's a girl who went to our school who died the night

after I was admitted to the hospital. I actually bumped into her right before my body collapsed."

"That girl who donated her hair to the cheerleaders?" Leif nodded in recognition.

"Yeah, Jessica Chai."

Hearing my name brought pause. There, after standing at another girl's graveside, Vivian and Leif talked about me. They said my name.

"You think?"

"It makes sense. She's the right age and time frame and cause of death. But I don't know for sure. I guess I like to think it was her because our lives crossed. Maybe only accidentally, maybe just that once, but she saw me and I saw her. Is that weird?"

"No weirder than the reality of having someone else's parts inside you."

"Your leg was rebuilt with donated materials, right?"

"Yes, though at the time they didn't tell me exactly what that meant."

Cadaver tissue, anyone? My tissue.

"Would you have refused? If you'd known?"

"No, but . . . I don't think so. . . . Look, I don't know anything about being a patient like you. I know that. But I do know about how life changes in an instant."

"Your injury?"

Leif nodded, his lips twisting in part frown, part grin. "It wasn't an accident. There's a guy in jail for it."

"What? You never told me—"

He interrupted. "Is it terrible that I want to thank him?"

Confusion snaked through Vivian's words. "Thank him?"

Huh? Thank him?

"Yeah, it's almost like he did me a favor."

"How?"

"I didn't have choices. I didn't know who I was. What I wanted. I didn't know you." Leif touched her leg.

Leif heard the rumors almost immediately after he woke in the hospital. A few of his teammates visited him, and then more came during his rehabilitation. They egged him on to seek vengeance when he was better. His injury was bought and paid for by a rival quarterback's family. The rationale? Leif received too many scout visits; scouts couldn't be in two places at once and weren't going to West Sealth's games in favor of Leif's. Their son was ignored because Leif garnered so much attention. Take Leif out, get noticed more. *Sick*.

"But how?"

"They paid off a lineman."

"How could anyone do that?"

"The kid's family was broke, I guess. They thought it wouldn't be that big a deal for me to get a little surgery, be out for the rest of the season. They seemed to think it was kind to not do it first game in September." His chin dipped with sadness.

"A little surgery? What? Four operations?"

Leif shrugged. "I was on autopilot. You are too."

"What are you talking about?" Vivian mustered taller in the seat.

"You're expecting a certain outcome."

"I am?"

"What college are you going to?"

She rolled her eyes. "I don't know."

"What's your wedding look like?"

"I don't know."

"Where are you buying a house and when are you starting a family?"

"I don't know!" Vivian's voice got louder and louder.

He smacked the steering wheel to prove his point. "See! You refuse to think about it. Most people think about it."

"I can't think about it."

"You don't want to. There's a difference."

"Why think about things that will never happen?"

"They won't if you don't want them, and work toward them, and put energy into making them happen," Leif vehemently argued, but it sounded like a lecture.

"My life isn't a football game, Coach."

"That's not what I'm saying. You're misunderstanding."

"No, actually I think I understand perfectly. You want me to have a winning attitude about this disease, but what you don't get is that the CF wins. Every freakin' time. CF, not me. Not Sally. Not Brian, or Crystal, or Wallace. Get it? They are *dead*. With transplants, or without transplants, it doesn't matter. None of them were eighty-two when they died." Vivian's eyes brimmed with unshed pain. *What does she call the color filling her whole body? Fear? Sadness? Depression? Failure?*

"Vivi—" Leif paled as she flinched away from his outstretched hand.

"Thanks, Coach, great talk." Vivian slammed the car door behind her, then the house door.

He knocked but she refused to answer.

She found more tears.

So did I.

CHAPTER TWENTY-THREE

Misty left the library early so she could get to school before the busses arrived. She wanted to see for herself if her hunch was correct.

Yep, I'm your donor. Why aren't you taking better care of my piece?

The idea that a stranger had saddled her with this existence was one thing. But to think that she'd seen me alive was too much to bear.

She passed the bathroom where she usually ate lunch and where she had hidden out during that fourth period last October.

At the end of the hallway, she stopped. Her feet stuck to the floor as if all of this year's old chewing gum was cheek to cheek between here and there.

She muttered. I felt her try to summon courage. The last drops of bravery squeezed from my liver and she moved forward.

Toward the trophy case. One foot in front of the other.

What happens to me next school year? When school is out for the summer, will they take all this down?

My photo stared back at us with as much personality as the paper it was printed on. Who was that girl? I no longer recognized her. No longer bound by my hair, or my body, or my thoughts of tomorrow. Tangled up in other people's breaths, and dreams, and pains. Next to my photo was the tacky, plastic, gold trophy the Skirts won for the hair drive.

Rage wanted to wash over me but Misty was drowning in a sea of depression, without purpose or direction. Misty's emptiness trumped anything the Skirts did to me.

Misty laid her hand against the glass, hoping to feel warmth, or welcome, or recognition. But all she felt was the hard, smooth glass. It told her no one cared. It lied.

I care! Sam cares! Your brother cares!

I was afraid that even if she physically heard me, even if I manifested and shouted in her face, she wouldn't, or couldn't, hear me in her heart.

What did that say about me? What did people think about my death?

Do I have the strength to face it all?

Her fear almost shoved my own away. But maybe, just maybe, if I turned toward the case and read the words written about me, she too would gain strength to face her life. I wanted lungs to sigh, and eyelids to force wide, and a brain to tell to read. But I was no longer there, no longer a piece of this world.

But when Misty began to read, her lips moving silently, I read too.

Jessica Frances Chai

Immensely talented and full of verve, Jessica Frances Chai had that rare je ne sais quoi the world envied. Born May 16, 1998, to parents Madeline Carlton-Chai and Richard Frances Chai, she is also survived by a brother, Carlton Chai, age ten. As an early philanthropist, in kindergarten her lemonade-stand proceeds went to the local food bank. Her annual trick-or-treating for UNICEF set the foundation of her character. Days prior to her death on November 1, Jessica donated her naturally platinum, waist-length locks to a children's cancer charity, making her school's Spirit Team winners in a crosstown competition. She changed the world during her too-short lifetime and asked us, too, to be better than we are.

She lives on in all our hearts and will be missed.

A scholarship for young philanthropists has been set up in her name and donations can be made at any Seattle's Bank branch or online.

Who wrote this? I don't know this Jessica Frances Chai. She's a stranger. Mother couldn't let me be. I had a lemonade stand once when I was five, but I lasted only a couple of hours because selling required talking to neighbors and strangers. That freaked me out. The only money I made was a buck from my father. I never donated to the food bank. Carlton does the UNICEF thing, not me. Ever. Change the world? How? Seriously, my mother wrote this with her bridge club and tennis partners in mind. Did anyone really know me? Ever?

I forgot about Misty until the tug of her moving away dragged me back to reality. She hurried off.

She headed for the bathroom.

She remembers seeing me.

Misty slunk into the girls' bathroom. She hadn't been inside this one since that day. That day, right after the Skirts hacked my hair and I ran into the bathroom to see how badly I was mutilated.

Misty beelined for the far stall.

I stayed by the mirror.

Her usual bathroom refuge had been out of service that week, so she'd hid in this one instead. Misty shut and locked the door. She covered the toilet seat thick with paper covers and sat down. Leaned forward against the wall, bracing herself so she could pick her feet up. Then she peered out the tiny gap between the stall supports and wall. Tiny, but big enough to see whoever stood in front of the mirror. Exactly like that day she saw me, but only in her memory. When she started crying, she buried her head in her sweatshirt to muffle the sobs.

"I'm so sorry. So sorry," Misty repeated.

It's not your fault.

Not then.

Not now.

CHAPTER TWENTY-FOUR

Samuel's sour food soured his mood, or maybe it was the text from his cousin that launched him into bad-mood orbit.

"Don't know her. Get last name?"

If he knew Misty's last name, he'd have included it in his message. He rubbed his neck; the knots in his shoulders were his own fault for spending hours hunched over.

His cousin Rebecca went to the same school I had. She was my postcard locker neighbor. The more these lives unfolded, the more I realized how utterly connected we all were. How related.

"Dammit!" Sam tossed his phone behind him without looking.

"Honey? Are you okay?" his ma called from the other side of the bedroom door. "Is everything all right?"

"I'm fine."

"Because I'm here if you need to talk or—"

"I'm fine!" Samuel's shout reverberated. He felt bad, but not bad enough to spend the next hour making up things she could give him advice about to feel useful.

She tiptoed off.

He clicked through his music library and cranked Rammstein's latest. It suited his mood, but hurt my ears.

When PigskinPaint pinged Samuel, he was beyond ready for the interruption.

```
PP: got time?
S: y wanna chat
   shoot
PP: my girl hates me
S: theres a lot of that going around
```

Samuel touched the origami crane he'd folded with Misty and wondered if he'd ever hear from her again.

```
PP: you got a girl?
S: dont know
   she hates me
PP: maybe in the water supply?
S: terrorism looks an awful like PMS?
PP: something like that
    what'd you do?
S: who says I did anything?
PP: we're always wrong
S: true
   tried to help her
PP: bad move
S: tell me about it
   u?
PP: tried to tell her
    she isn't going to die young
S: she suicidal?
```

PP: nah
    I don't think so
    just has a thing that can't be cured
    seems like she's given up
S: bad day or in general?
PP: we went to her friend's funeral
S: a Darwinism huh?
PP: what you mean?
S: the natural order of things
   makes even the most scholarly of faithful
   question interference
   in either science
   or God's will
PP: my SAT score just went up reading that
    but explain it in English
S: i should be dead
   if medicine hadnt intervened I would be
   does that make it intervention
   a miracle
   or something else?
PP: can't it be all three and then some?
    do you have to know?
S: ah
   but if u dont know which it is
   how do you accept when others arent saved
   or fixed
   or cured?
   what makes u special and them not?
PP: how do u deal with it then?

S: still learning
   but it comes with a lot of responsibility
   there are all these people out there who are
   hoping i live up
   to the potential of their dead person
   its a lot of pressure.
PP: even if the dead guy wasn't going to be
    president
    or a nobel prize winner?
S: people have a weird way of making the dead
   into saints
   happens everywhere
   across cultures & religions

Tell me about it. Philanthropist? Really?

PP: like ignoring how much he pissed you off
    or that he owed you money
S: y
   people make up shit to feel better
   about wasting time
PP: that's what we fought about
S: what?
PP: wasting time
    she's convinced she's going to die young
    and shouldn't think about the future
S: i understand this
PP: how?
    cuz i don't

        she's got a new chance
        more time
S: before i had surgery odds werent good
    id see the next decade
    let alone my 80th birthday
PP: now?
S: theres middle ground
    we can all die today
    for a million different reasons
    dying young can happen to anyone except the
    old
PP: that sounds like a fortune cookie
S: i have that tendency
    look
    its hard to want more than u already have
    when u know people whod give anything
    for a minute with a dead kid
    maybe she feels guilty about making plans
    because they cant
PP: thnx
      that helps
S: can i ask you a favor?
PP: sure
S: u live in Seattle
    right?
PP: y
S: u ever heard of East Sealth High?
PP: that's my school
S: no way

```
PP: true
    why
S: do u know a girl named Misty?
   my cuz also goes there but she doesnt know
   her
```

Sam sat back and waited while the cursor blinked. There were no coincidences. He knew this, but he still startled when he saw the connections in action. Of course PigskinPaint Leif goes to Misty's school. In Samuel's mind, the world eased into another degree of connectedness.

Of course?

```
PP: sorry man
    i don't know Misty
    what's your cuz's name?
S: Rebecca Sabir
PP: nope
    my mom has the yearbooks
    I can go ask her for them right now
S: nah
   dont worry about it
PP: sounds important
S: im worried about her
   i thought maybe since u went to the same
   school
   u might know her
   shes in bad shape
   had a liver transplant
```

```
                i think the whole thing is messing with her
                head
                my cuz is looking
PP: u want me to track misty down?
S: i hate to ask that
   but
PP: not a problem man
     it'll give me a reason to talk to Viv 2
     maybe she knows her
S: thnx
   just keep showing her theres a reason to
   plan the future
   its about looking ahead not down
PP: true
S: u any closer to figuring out whether u
   want to play ball this fall?
PP: no man
     I've made up my mind not to
     but then my parents are counting on me
     idk
```

Samuel tapped a few keys and sent a fresh message to another Seattle friend, then clicked back into his conversation with Leif.

```
S: i want u to go by Saint's Rehab
   ask for Pirate
PP: why?
    who's Pirate?
```

S: hes a friend
   met him online 2
   i told him youll be stopping by
   i think hes good for your questions
PP: dude u sound like a motivational speaker
    and u suck

   Samuel laughed. Maybe.
   I totally agree.

S: sure   .
   just go see him
   ill message u the addy
   consider it a favor
PP: you're not setting me up on a date r u?
S: no
   no date
   wouldnt want to break Vivs heart
PP: Haha
    pretty sure she hates me
S: nah
   shes a girl
   girls r weird
PP: that's profound
    and jackass
S: true
   but am i wrong?
   go meet Pirate
   & report back
PP: aye aye

CHAPTER TWENTY-FIVE

The door to the bathroom swung open and Misty instinctively held her breath. But between the sniffing and nose trumpeting, it didn't take long for her to blow her cover.

"Are you okay?" Patent leather sneakers with pink laces stopped in front of the stall door. "Are you crying?"

"No, I'm fine," Misty answered, hoping she'd go away.

"Are you sure? I think I have tissues in my locker. I can run and get them. Oh, wait, I think they're in my bag." The girl bent down and Misty listened to her riffle through her backpack. A couple of pens fell out, along with three postcards that flew under the stall like they were on strings.

"Oops," she said, but held a packet of tissues with cats on them under the door. "Trade you, if you can grab those."

Misty saw a hippo riding a bike, some stone temple in a jungle, and a bright blue frog as she scooped the postcards up and handed them back under.

"Thanks!"

The girl made sure Misty took the tissues before she tossed everything back into her bag and moved away. "My locker is right out there. If you wanna talk or—"

"Sure," Misty replied, but offered nothing else.

"Okay, see ya."

Misty realized she hadn't thanked the girl or asked her name.

Rebecca. Her name is Rebecca, and she's looking for you.

CHAPTER TWENTY-SIX

Leif was up all night reading a medical textbook on cystic fibrosis. He memorized terms and treatments like he used to do with football drills and plays. Next on his weekend agenda was meeting up with Pirate. Samuel was the only guy Leif confided in. So far Sam hadn't laughed, or made him feel stupid. That went a long way in Leif's mind.

The rehabilitation center was about an hour's drive south, set right outside the joint military bases. Sam refused to tell Leif anything useful about who Pirate was, or why Leif was there to see him.

Leif walked into Saint's and approached the front desk. *Like there's another option?* "Hi, um, what room is Pirate in?"

"What's your name?"

"Leif Leolin. MiracleMan Samuel sent me?"

And the receptionist doesn't even bat an eyelash? Cool place.

"He's probably in the gym. Hang on. Have a seat." She picked up the phone and started dialing.

The rehab center looked like a huge house but with lots of medical equipment and machines in corners, nooks, and the steady movement of an overcapacity anthill.

"Hey, kid."

I saw the speaker at the same time Leif focused on him. Tough and wiry, he exuded warrior. *Pirate?*

"Hi, I'm Leif." Leif stuck out his hand, then let it drop when he saw the gloves and pressure bandages up and down Pirate's right side, visible under a tank top and running shorts. Pirate was missing pieces.

"Pirate." The man held out his left fist to bump.

The two shiny question marks where his legs used to be immediately grabbed Leif's attention. "Cool blades." Leif nodded toward the prosthetics with his chin.

"You got your sneakers on?" Pirate was already moving. I got the feeling sitting still was not in his repertoire.

"Yes, sir," Leif answered, feeling as though he'd inadvertently signed up for boot camp.

"Good, let's run." Pirate waved at the woman on the desk and then headed out the front door. "So, I hear you aren't sure you want to do football in the fall. Want to be a painter or singer instead."

Was there anything Sam left out? I smiled, or tried to, anyway. *Leif's pretty cute when he's embarrassed.*

"Don't worry, kid, I'm good at asking questions to get information."

Leif nodded. The pace pushed his muscles. He'd forgotten how much he enjoyed the burn of working out past his wall. "Sure. How long have you been running on those?" He pointed down at the prosthetics.

"Months. I'm working up to the Iron Man. Burns take a while to heal and skin grafts come in stages."

"The Iron Man?" Shock reverberated through Leif.

"It's about self-discipline. You any good?"

"At football?"

"Or the singing? What are you good at?"

"They think I can go pro at quarterback."

"Ah, that's a lot of responsibility."

"It is?"

"Sure it is. Leading your team on the field. All those players trying to take you down. Not for the faint of heart. What about singing?"

"I suck."

"How long do you work at it?"

"Hours."

"You feel better when you're singing or on the field?"

"I hadn't thought about it like that."

"You should try. It's a shame to do something every day that doesn't make you want to keep going. I'm grateful. Every breath. It's sappy, but it's truth. Sometimes it takes an injury to find that."

"Yeah?"

Pirate held up his hand and showed Leif his fused fingers. "I'd be back out there in a second, kid. With my men. Heading into the field of combat. It's where I belong, it's what drives me. Before this? I thought about getting out, going back to school, becoming an accountant or some shit."

"And that changed?"

"Yes." Pirate stopped. "I can't carry a pack yet. This body is now a liability to my soldiers. I'm not going out into combat again. Not soon. But I can teach them everything I learned, everything that got me through that day, and the eight years of missions before it. I'm not a pencil pusher, not in this body before, and not now. Let me ask you this. Who's gonna die if you don't take the field?"

Leif snorted. "I know it's not the same thing—"

"Which gives you way more room to try things and make choices. Right? So you might make some poor girl's ears bleed until you figure out you're a painter, not a singer. Or maybe you'll miss the football field come September. But you've got a choice. No one's gonna die. They might yell at you, but you stay standing and you'll find your path."

"Why are you doing the Iron Man? Why not just do regular workouts?"

"My son saw me and asked his mother if I'd be able to play hide-and-seek again. He didn't know I was listening. I'm doing the Iron Man for me. But I'm really learning to run on these things for my kid. Hard to hide a hospital bed and a wheelchair from a six year old. You up for four more miles?"

"Sure." Leif pounded out next to Pirate.

Leif logged in as soon as he got home to tell Samuel about hanging out with Pirate.

```
PP: u there?
S: chat @ me
PP: exactly what i needed
S: cool
    hes awesome
    isnt he?
```

```
PP: y
      made me want to be him
S: oh hell man
    u r not enlisting
    r u?
```

For what, the bad singer battalion? Or the finger-painting special-ists? Boys.

```
PP: thought about it
      but only 4 a sec
S: not tough enough huh?
PP: nope
      total wuss
      u were right man
      he taught me a lot
      and ran the shit out of me
S: hes a good guy
PP: so what happened
      to him?
S: u didnt ask
PP: didn't seem polite
S: dug up the story online
    & saw his commendation paperwork in a file
PP: isn't that illegal hacking?
S: only if you dont use it for good
PP: right
      what'd u find out?
S: he survived a night ambush
    he held off a dozen insurgents alone
```

```
        he was the only conscious member of his team
        was shot in the legs and through his hand
        but only one wounded guy died
        & he was shot in the head early
        nothing Pirate could have done to save him
PP: wow
S: theres more
PP: corse there is
S: as he was rescued
        convoy hit an IED
        thats when he lost the legs & got so burned
PP: that's horrific
S: true
        but when i asked him about it he said
        at least it got rid of the bullet holes
PP: that's one way to see it
S: thats the point
PP: what is?
S: always more than one way of seeing things
        good or bad
```

Huh, maybe so.

```
PP: oh hey mom gave me the yrbooks
        i now have a pic of your Misty
        i think
        there r 2
        but one grad last year
        do u know her last name?
```

S: not yet

   i havent asked

   cuz I didnt want to come off as 2 cyberstalker

PP: good point

   r u in prison?

S: N

PP: r u a politician

   hunting up young boys

   to seduce with your power?

S: N

PP: r u a cult leader looking for slaves

   to sell to your followers?

S: hell man where r u coming up with this
   stinking load?

PP: i've been working on a lot of songs

   imagination is bulking up

S: is that what u call it?

PP: screw u

CHAPTER TWENTY-SEVEN

Misty accidentally found herself in the apartment with her mother. Alone. Her papa was out looking for work; her grandmother was down at the corner market checking for her special imported fish. Her brother was at a piano lesson.

Mama flinched and rubbed her right shoulder, grabbing Misty's attention.

How long had she been hurt?

"Hand me the big bowl from above the fridge?" her mama asked.

"Mama, are you hurt?" Misty dragged the heavy ceramic bread bowl onto the counter.

She didn't answer, but nodded slightly.

Misty pushed. "Your arm?"

"Shoulder." Mama moved the bowl but favored her hurt arm considerably.

"You need to see a doctor, don't you?"

"No, it'll be fine."

"But how do you work?" The daily quotas her mother was expected to meet meant working the line at top speed for the full shift.

"It's fine."

"Mama—"

"Don't." Her mother raised her voice.

Misty shrank back.

Oh, Misty, this isn't your fault.

"I will see doctors soon."

"We don't have money, do we?" Misty asked.

"It's always tight."

"But especially now, because of me." Misty didn't ask. She knew.

"Your papa is handling it. He says we're close to paying them all off."

Misty glanced around the apartment, seeing all the things that were missing.

There was no television. Her brother's game system gone. Her mother's crystal vase from the ancestors gone. As was her mother's gold wedding band.

"Did he sell your ring?"

"No, I lost it," Mama answered, but Misty didn't believe her.

"Mama—"

"I will pick up your medicines for this month when I get paid tomorrow."

"No!" Misty jerked away. If she hadn't stopped taking the meds every day to make them last longer, she'd already be out of pills. As it was, she alternated kinds and skipped days. So far, she felt no ill effects.

I notice changes. Why doesn't anyone else?

"What? Why not?" Mama looked up, concern, worry, and stress evident in every extra line framing her features.

Please ask. Please demand to see the bottles. Please notice!

Misty lied quickly. "I already got them."

"How did you pay?"

"I got a job."

"You did? When?"

"A couple of weeks ago."

"Where?"

"At the library. After school, before classes too."

"You get paid enough for the medicines?" Her mama was dubious. Something had to feel wrong to her about Misty's answers. Wrong with the way she acted. The way she was quiet, and tired, and not as pilled-up puffy, should make her family notice.

"Yes, and school fees, the college preparatory tests too." Misty knew by mentioning college, her mama's attention could be diverted.

"Good. That's a help. Your papa will be proud you are working. But your grades are high, yes? Still top of the class?"

Misty never showed her parents her report cards. In the beginning, years ago, they didn't understand or read them. When she began getting average, and mediocre, reports, she simply told them what they wanted to hear. "Yes."

They're too busy surviving to know what to ask for. And she's too busy surviving each breath to know to ask for help.

CHAPTER TWENTY-EIGHT

Vivian tossed her charcoal pencil onto the table in frustration. There were two subjects relentlessly seeking creation: Leif's face. The perfect prom dress.

Leif wanted her to be perky and optimistic, and the only way she knew how to do that was to live in a certain amount of denial. If she didn't make plans, she never faced disappointment. It worked for her. His loss.

Yours. Mainly yours.

Until she saw the signs for prom and a spark of hope flickered. She didn't care about prom. It represented normal high school. A life she never had.

She trudged over to the half-finished self-portrait and stared at it.

"I'm sorry I got all motivational speaker on you."

Vivian jumped. "Jesus! I didn't hear you."

My heart thumped and galloped. *She's happy to see him.*

"Sorry," Leif said. "You were pretty engrossed. You going to finish it?"

Vivian turned from the canvas and shuffled her sketches

together. The last thing she wanted Leif to see were the forty-seven drawings of his eyes, of him in a tux, of him dancing with a girl. She knew better than to believe in fairy tales. "Maybe."

"I wish you would."

"What are you doing here?" She flinched at the harsh sound of her voice.

"I wish you weren't so mad at me."

"I'm not mad."

Leif nodded, but we all knew it was a lie. "I'm sorry. I care about you."

Vivian snorted. "If you care about me so much, why are you going to prom with Karly?

Leif rocked back on his heels. "Who?"

"Senior? Built like a lingerie model?"

"I'm not going to prom." He shook his head. His expression told Vivian he had no idea where this came from, but she didn't see it.

Poor guy, he wonders if he missed an entire conversation.

"Right." Jealousy began creeping in (Pantone 12-5204), then strengthened (Pantone 345) and quickly grew dark and ugly (Pantone 18-0119).

"I'm not. Prom's dumb."

Vivian stomped over and shoved her pens and paper in the bag. "My break is over. I have to get back to work."

"Sure." Leif licked his lips. "But wait, are you mad that I'm not going to prom or that I didn't ask you?"

"You said yourself that prom is dumb."

"You wanted to go, didn't you?"

Before the transplant, it never would have occurred to her to hope for an invitation. But after the transplant, after Leif limped into her life, she wanted more.

Life divides into BT and AT. Before Transplant. After Transplant.

"Hi, Leif!" Cassidy barreled into the back room. "Haven't seen you recently." She stuttered to a stop. "Um, Vivian, I don't know how to explain fused etching"—she dropped her voice—"and this customer has to know *now*."

"Sure." Vivian nodded. "I have to work." She followed Cassidy into the main store.

Leif must have let himself out the back, because even though Vivian pretended to be spectacularly busy, she never saw him leave.

CHAPTER TWENTY-NINE

Misty climbed the stairs to her little nook and waited several moments, trying to catch her breath and stop the room from spinning. She felt woozy. She had to tell Samuel. The need to confide overcame the desire to hide. Surrounded by her flock of paper cranes, she logged in to see if he was waiting.

```
M: Sam?
S: im here
   wanna chat?
```

Misty inhaled and said a quick prayer that she wouldn't lose her nerve.

```
M: have to tell u something
S: ok
S: Misty?
M: mom hurt her shoulder
   and she won't go to the doctor
S: is she afraid of doctors?
```

```
M: no
   we can't afford it
S: sucks
   sorry
M: ALL my fault
   the hospital bills and the surgery stuff
   and the medicines I have to take
   there's no money
```

Misty hurt all over. Her bones felt heavy and her muscles weak. Maybe she had the flu. Maybe she was getting what she deserved. *No one deserves this.*

Sam dinged back fast and furiously.

```
S: do they tell you its your fault?
   cuz thats bullshit
   total shit
M: no
```

The silence of the blinking cursor tortured Samuel. He needed video. He needed voice. He needed to see her, the real her, and reassure her. There was more. Certainty gripped him.

```
S: tell me more
```

Misty sipped from a bottle of water she'd refilled in the bathroom sink. She left the top off because it was too hard to screw back on.

M: i lied to my mom
S: ok
   about?
M: told her i got a job and
   paying for my pills
S: &?
M: i check the mail and take the bills out
   it's not like i want to get away with not
   paying
   it's just that they get so stressed
   and fight
S: &?
M: i think maybe something is wrong with me
S: why?
M: my stomach hurts

And your pee is a weird orange-brown color. I wonder what Vivian would Pantone it.

S: only yr stomach?
M: no
   i'm really tired
   all the time
S: isnt school almost over?

I watched Samuel struggle to find words of comfort or optimism. His own stomach hurt trying to cross the distance. He had no idea what to say.

Pretty sure she isn't listening anyway.

```
M: soon
S: so u get the summer off
   right?
   u can rest?
M: no
   i will be watching a bunch of neighbors' kids
   during the day again this summer
S: what?
```

Surrounded by kid germs was the last place she should be.
Samuel wanted to throttle her parents for not getting it. I wanted
to join him for a long list of grievances.

```
M: free child care
   i do it every summer and vacation
   i owe them
S: who
M: family
S: U R not a slave Misty
M: i no
S: u need to go talk to your transplant doctor
   or go to the emergency room
   & u have to take your pills
   all of them
   all of the time
M: it's a handful
   they make me gag
   they make my stomach do flips and twists
   i hate them
```

```
S: they keep your body from rejecting the liver
   they r vital
```

Vital as in will die without them. The need to stand up overcame Misty, so she cradled another handful of cranes and tucked them into the spines of thick books and into the odd spaces on the shelves between books of varying sizes. Cranes from baby-size to giant adorned every empty surface.

Samuel waited, staring at the screen. Hoping she hadn't logged off, that he hadn't pushed too hard for her to take care of herself.

```
S: Misty?
M: here
S: do u feel guilty because u got sick?
M: i know who my donor was
   she went to my school
S: r u sure?
M: i saw her a couple days before she died
   and she was so upset
   she'd gotten a bad haircut and I ignored her
   i stayed in the bathroom stall
   and watched her cry
   and didn't try to help her
   18r i heard her hair was cut as a joke
```

You didn't want me to see your pain. You were hiding too.

```
S: do u know how to cut hair?
M: no
```

```
but I could have offered to give her
tissues or something
told her it wasn't so bad
that she'd survive at least
I hid from her instead
```

And you needed someone to say all of those same things to you. You can't give what you don't have.

Samuel knew he had to change the subject. Get her thinking about something other than the crushing guilt and insignificance she seemed to drown in. He said a quick prayer that he might say the right words, find the way to reach Misty, comfort her from so far away.

```
S: have i ever told you about my addiction
   to snail mail?
M: no
S: i will send you a postcard
   what's your mailing addy?
M: why?
S: i like real mail
   it stays around when the power goes out
M: do u wonder what stays here
   when our power goes out?
S: r u afraid of death?
M: yes
```

Misty couldn't imagine, but knew she'd be even more alone dead than she was living.

```
S: what scares u most?
M: not no-ing
S: u cant know until u believe
M: what?
S: u have to believe in it
   B 4 u can understand
   u have to believe there will be a net 2 catch
   u before u jump
M: i don't know if i can do that
```

Samuel's frustration overcame him. He didn't have the words. He saw a shrinking window of opportunity with Misty. She was giving up. He felt it. He couldn't make her hang on but God could. Why was He letting her suffer like this? Believing that her family would be better off if she died. Terrified of death because her present loneliness was all she saw of the beyond.

"Come on, speak to her. Show her. Make her believe in you," Samuel called out. He tried to pray, but God wasn't listening. He felt that too. As if God decided Sam used up all his prayers and miracles on himself. Like that friend who turned his back because too much was asked of the friendship.

```
M: i have 2 go
S: Misty?
   promise me u will log back in tomorrow
M: sure
S: no
   really
   promise me
M: i promise
```

Samuel scoured the web for examples of faith in action. He wanted to prove to Misty she had to hold on. He hunted for her donor. His own search went on hold.

Bingo.

THE SEATTLE TIMES
November 3

Local Teen Jessica Chai Turned Tragedy into the Ultimate Gift

Her parents said, "She was always talking about how she was going to change the world." And in the most profound way, she did. It will be months before her family is fully notified how many donors and lives she changed. As of this article, there are four known organ recipients, but cornea and tissue recipients have not yet been reported back.

The transplant coordinator's office was very forthcoming about organ and tissue donation, especially for children and teens. "Many of the children waiting for organs need the organs of other children because of their specialized size. Parents don't often think about the unexpected death of a child, so they're faced with the decision to donate at the same moment they're trying to accept a tragedy and say good-bye. It's heartbreaking."

The mother of an infant who donated her baby's organs, successively saving five other babies, told us, "When a child dies, and parents do not donate, there are multiple tragedies. I would do anything to save other parents from what I'm feeling. Nothing will bring back my baby, but knowing that there are five children growing up who could have died too? There is a peace, in knowing they have futures, I wouldn't have otherwise. There is peace. I don't understand why more parents don't donate."

In a world where teenagers are most often talked about as thinking themselves immortal and untouchable, Jessica Chai was an anomaly. By talking to her parents about her desires to be an organ donor, she made this an easy decision. Her mother insisted, "This wasn't our decision, we're just following her wishes. She even posted her pledge to her social media accounts."

The list of needed donations goes beyond the usual heart, liver, and kidneys. Other lesser-known tissue donations are: skin used for grafts on burn patients, bones used to rebuild joints and jaws of those injured in accidents or facing cancer, as well as veins and arteries that can restore limb function. The list goes on—one donor can outright save the lives of a dozen people and improve the quality of life for fifty more. And yet, every year the list of those who need grows greater. Thousands of people die each year waiting for a lifesaving decision. That's a staggering loss of life that could be saved.

Cheerleaders at Jessica's high school are putting together a memorial case and will hold a pep assembly to educate the student body about her gifts.

"We're all totally supportive of Jessica. It's really sad. She was in my math class in seventh grade," offered Tiffany Jones.

Perhaps Jessica's decision will spur other families to have conversations and make pledges. Though overcome with grief, Jessica's father did add, "We hope she'll be remembered as the giving person she always was. Carlton can be proud of his big sister."

Samuel sat back and stared at the screen. I started reading from the top. Again. And again.

Leif jotted down, erased, crossed off, and ultimately started a new page. He wanted to fix things with Vivian. He was inspired by their early conversations about seeing potential donors doing reckless acts and making ill-conceived choices. He wanted her to know he was listening. He'd paid attention. She mattered to him.

He strummed a chord and sang, "Oh, no, there goes a donor . . ."

He tried again. "Dead-man-walking donor . . . Stupid-stunt-girl donor . . ."

Leif sighed. Songwriting wasn't as easy as passing the ball. But he was tired of easy. He wanted real. Vivian was the realest part of his life.

He flipped through his notebook and looked at the title of his first love song. "Vivian."

He tapped a beat on the guitar and sang a cappella, "She sees the world in color, in universal colors . . . who names the colors, feels and sees and breathes the colors."

Just sing songs already written. You have a nice voice, but you suck at writing lyrics.

Leif paused and began working on the next lines. "'Her strength is . . .' What rhymes with *inspirational?*"

He skipped over verses and tried to match sound and chords to the chorus. YouTube made it look so easy.

"Confident, sexy, vibrant Vivian . . ."

". . . Lovely, funny, pretty Vivian . . ."

This is painful. Yet of the four of them, at the moment, he's the least painful.

Samuel had his head buried in religious texts, trying to find answers for Misty. Misty was curled up in her library den, barely managing to make a couple of cranes an hour. Vivian kept scraping the canvases free of paint and starting over.

They're a mess.

Leif's message alert dinged and he saw MiracleMan Sam's ID pop up with a message.

S: u around? 911

Leif put the guitar down and typed a quick response.

PP: what's up?
S: i think Misty is bad sick
   im afraid she might do crazy

She doesn't have the strength to be crazy.

```
PP: do what?
S: idk
   suicide
PP: wow
    true?
S: IDK
   she gave me her address
   i dont have my license but im going to
   hitch up there
   can i crash with u for a night?
   rather the fam not know im in town
   2 many ???s
PP: don't hitch
    if u r afraid of time u need 2 fly
    can u catch a flight?
S: im tapped
   sent all cash to the charities already this
   month
   or id borrow it
```

Leif looked at the sixty bucks in his basketball-shaped bank from elementary school. He didn't have enough either.

```
PP: people get raped and murdered hitching
S: nah i think u just have to be careful
   i will pick minivans or soccer moms
PP: im pretty sure they don't stop
S: i gotta try man
   i gotta try
```

```
PP: hold tight
    don't go anywhere
    give me time to see if I can't get u a ticket
S: im not asking u to cover it
   but im good for it
PP: im not worried
    i have 2 ask Viv
    so give me an hour to get back to u
    ok?
S: sure
   gotta finish laundry nywy
   or my ma will know sums up
```

Come on, Leif. Leif grabbed the car keys and headed toward Art and Soul. His parents were out running and hopefully he'd be back before they noticed. I didn't know if saving Misty was possible, but if Samuel and Leif tried, if they noticed her pain, maybe that would save her heart.

Leif waved at Cassidy when he entered.

She smiled. "She's still mad at you. But between you and me, I don't think it's mad." Cassidy lowered her voice as other customers walked in.

"What is it, then?" Leif asked, genuinely intrigued. He needed the insight.

"Fear. Of you deciding you prefer blond cheerleader babes over artists. It's an unwritten rule that the quarterback dates the head cheerleader."

He shook his head. "Funny, I didn't get that rule book."

"Like I said, it's unwritten." She grinned.

"She's not here, is she?"

"Nope, at home, moping."

"Okay, thanks." He turned to go. At least he knew where she lived. He checked the time as he left.

"Hey, Leif?" Cassidy called out.

He stopped and turned. "Yeah?"

"Take flowers. She likes sweet peas—they have some at the market today."

"Thanks." Leif mentally detoured. If sweet peas might get her to listen, then he'd get flowers.

CHAPTER THIRTY

Vivian missed him. She was used to carrying around grief, but because that friend was dead, not because she chose not to be with him. This was new and she didn't like it at all. She finished hanging the self-portrait above her bed.

Before transplant. After transplant.

She liked it. Vivian left one side of her face blank, with the merest smudges of shadow and feature. Her future was blank and it was her choices that would fill it up, not the cystic fibrosis.

The other side of her face she'd intricately painted with tiny portraits of those she'd outlived, the bits of experiences and mementos that kept her going even when she wanted to give up. She was two halves in one lifetime.

She stepped back and finished unpacking her hospital luggage. The next time she packed these bags she would be going to the airport and heading out on a grand adventure. Not going in for a biopsy. From now on, for medical, she'd take a toothbrush and a pair of pajamas with her. No longer would she bide her time between physical breakdowns; she refused to calculate her life by appointments anymore. Tomorrow, she and her mom would go shopping for a prom dress. Just for fun.

When the doorbell rang, Vivian hoped for a second it was Leif. But she had no idea where to begin repairing the damage or how to explain that the buttons he'd pushed were the most painful. She took her time, assuming it was a UPS delivery or a kid selling candy for summer camp.

It *was* Leif. Vivian's mouth went dry and she gripped the banister so she wouldn't fall.

Yep, Prince Charming is here. Open the door.

He pressed the doorbell again and the chime reverberated through the house.

"Hi." Vivian opened the front door and leaned against it.

"Look, I know you're mad at me. And you can yell at me or throw things or whatever later, but I need you to call a truce for a little while and help a friend."

She swung open the door. "I call truce if those sweet peas are for me."

"Oh, yeah." He thrust them forward. "Cassidy said they were your favorite."

"You went there?"

"You're usually working."

"Having a home day."

"So, I saw you with a credit card, right?"

"Romantic opener." She raised her eyebrows. "Yeah? So?"

Leif launched into the story of Sam and what he knew about Misty.

"Come on." Vivian dragged him up the stairs. "It sounds like she's rejecting the liver. You can't stop taking the meds, Leif, they're the only thing that keeps the body from turning on the organ. She's going to die if she doesn't get treatment." Vivian stopped.

Leif touched her shoulder. "What aren't you saying?"

Vivian filled with a hopeless bleakness (Pantone Cool Gray 7). "It might be too late if she's not getting checkups and tests. They monitor me so carefully. You've seen some of the pills I take."

"Those aren't for your CF? She'd need to take those too?"

"Most of them are for the transplants. People don't understand, Leif, but an organ transplant isn't the end of the story, it's the beginning."

It isn't the end, but the beginning? Why did that resonate so deeply within me? Was my end simply a new beginning?

"Can you loan me the money to get Samuel a plane ticket?"

"Consider it a gift. If she has a chance at this, she has to have all the support she can get."

They headed for the computer, and while Leif logged into MiracleMakers and pinged Samuel, Vivian pulled up a travel app on her tablet and checked for flights.

```
PP: u take off yet?
S: n
   packed
   any luck?
PP: Let me video chat u
    so u can talk to Viv 2
```

I was the only one who knew all four of these teens were connected, entwined by my pieces, connected by something bigger than me. It was odd seeing the three together, but much easier to keep track of all the events.

There are so many different ways to live each moment. Seeing them together brought that home for me. They made each second unique because it was theirs to live.

"Hi, Vivian." Samuel appeared worried and unkempt.

"Hi. How long will it take you to get to the airport?" she asked, without small talk.

"About ten minutes. Ma rented this house based on proximity for traveling."

"Good. So if you leave now, you might make it through security in time for the next flight."

Leif leaned in to the screen. "I'll meet you at the passenger exit at Sea-Tac."

"I don't know how to thank you guys—"

"Don't thank us." Vivian waved him off.

"We'll go to the address you gave us and see if she's home," Leif assured Samuel.

Sam shook his head. "I don't think she talked to me from home."

Vivian pulled up directions from her place to Misty's. "This isn't exactly a good neighborhood."

"They're really poor, I think. Her parents work all the time, and her grandmother doesn't speak any English."

"We'll try to find her first. But I'll definitely be at the airport, and we can hunt more if we need to."

"Thanks. I mean it."

"Okay, write this down. It's your confirmation number." Vivian rattled off the code.

Samuel signed off and Leif sat next to Vivian in silence, both of them lost in their thoughts.

"If she's really that sick, do you think he'll make it in time?" Leif asked.

"I don't know. I depends on how bad it is and if she wants to fight. Sounds like she's losing the mental battle." Vivian turned her hand over, palm up, in truce and invitation.

"Is that why you live so much in the moment?" Leif's fingers crept closer until their pinkies touched and twined.

"Looking ahead is exhausting. When parts start to fail, it feels like—" She broke off.

"Like what?"

"You ever see those dominoes competitions where they spend days setting up a bunch of lines and then one little nudge and in seconds they're all falling down?"

"Yeah?"

"I think sometimes it's like that inside me, and when one thing goes wrong, it's just a trigger for everything to start failing. And I can't see inside, so I don't know where to put my hand to fix it, or stop it, as if I'm along for a ride I don't control. It's going to end up with me dead sooner or later."

"If she feels out of control too—"

"She may not think there is any point in trying to stop the dominoes from falling." Vivian filled in the rest of the sentiment.

"I like the portrait." Leif pointed to the painting. "I like how you painted your future open for possibility."

"You see that?" Vivian asked, with no little awe.

"Isn't that what the blank part is?"

"Thank you."

"For what?"

"For getting me."

"I'll call you when I get to her apartment." Leif stood.

Vivian shook her head. "I'm going with you."

"No, you said yourself it's not the best neighborhood."

"All the more reason to not go alone. Besides, you don't know what she's going through, and I do."

Though he didn't look happy about it, Leif relented. "'Kay, let's go."

There were lots of words for Misty's part of town. *The ghetto. Projects. Hood. Working-class poverty.* But for Vivian it felt as if all the color had been sucked off everything and everyone, and left in shades of sepia tones (Pantone 16-1439 and 476). As if life were so demanding and unrelenting that even the colors were tired and droopy.

Cinder blocks and bricks, concrete and cracked pavement beckoned them into cramped hallways and even-more-crowded rooms.

Leif held Vivian's hand, and he was the one who knocked.

A young boy cracked the apartment door; his eye widened and he quickly opened the door, slipped out, and shut it behind him. "You know my sister?"

"We're trying to find her. To help her," Vivian answered.

"She's not here. She's spending a lot of time at the library."

"Is she sicker? Have you noticed anything?"

He nodded. "I don't think the transplant's working. She's not right. And I don't think she went to her last doctor visit. She told my parents she has a job, but she doesn't. She takes the mail away so they don't see the numbers. She said it was none of my business but . . ." His eyes filled with tears and his expression made him look years younger, a child on the verge of young adulthood, growing up too fast.

"We'll make it our business."

"Tell us, which library?" Vivian asked.

"I'll take you," George answered.

CHAPTER THIRTY-ONE

Helpless. Samuel tried to raise his eyes, but he just kept staring at his shoes. He left his ma a detailed note about his plans and then walked a mile down the road and caught a free hotel shuttle to the airport. He blended into the traveling crowd; no one asked if he was a guest at the hotel. He'd packed light, only a backpack with all his meds, a change of clothes, fresh boxers and socks, and a few of his favorite prayer books. He'd grabbed a collection of Navajo prayers, Psalms from the Bible, and Buddhist meditations to read on the plane.

When he collapsed into the window seat, Samuel prayed fervently that this aluminum contraption could defy logic and gravity and make it to Seattle without crashing.

He's not exactly a happy traveler. He's scared to death of flying.

Why had God brought Misty into his life, if not to save her? Samuel always felt God's presence, but tonight there was no relaxing in his faith. *And I hadn't seen God hanging around.*

What purpose brought Sam and Misty together if not to lift her up? He wrestled without answers, so he turned to a childhood trick of asking the question and flipping open a text to see God's answer.

Good question, but . . . weird.

Sam asked questions and randomly opened the texts. Over the years, he felt as though he found answers, strength, in the serendipity of unplanned words. He hesitated, hating the possibility he might read bad news; it was even hard to open the books.

He knew God's plan for him was special. That was why he kept a positive outlook. It was far easier to think that the unbearable was somehow reasonable if only he had all the information. He believed that if he'd died before the transplant, that would have served a purpose. His getting the organs served another purpose. He didn't usually need to know the details for his life, for his peace of mind, but tonight Samuel wanted details. Lots of details.

God remained silent.

The books gave no clear directions.

And even though I tried to speak, to touch his shoulder, to turn his overhead light off and on, my presence was unfelt too.

Misty waited at the computer for an hour. Where was he?

He's on a plane coming to rescue you.

She finished a crane, number 342, and tucked it high above the bookshelves, where it peeked down at the world below. What was it like to fly? To look down at all the suffering and stay above it? Misty wanted to come back in her next life as a crane. She saw the tartan-print crane nod at her and flap its wings in anticipation of taking off. It flew around the books and over her head before settling back into its nest.

She's hallucinating.

When Sam didn't answer, Misty wrote his name and email address on the outside of the bill binder, and rather than folding another crane, she picked up a pen and began a note. She wished it were a postcard, but the backside of the Story Time notice had to do.

Dear Samuel,

Misty paused, every thought taking crazy amounts of effort. Sweat dribbled down her back and along her hairline.

> *Thank you. You were a good friend to me. I have always felt so alone, you made the world less lonely. I wish I had your strength to fight, but I don't. I am sorry to disappoint you. More than you know. I have a favor. Please take care of my brother, George. He'll need a friend, a brother. He needs you to make sure he has fun and go hear him play the piano. He's a big brain, so smart he can do anything, but he'll need support. Teach him the things I can't. I'm afraid he'll give it up. Please tell these doctors I am dead and that my parents can't pay them. I hope they'll forgive me. All of them. Think of me when you see birds dancing in the clouds. That's where I am, swinging, flying high, free. Finally free. Forgive me for not being—*

She knows she's dying. She might not understand the mechanics or the processes or why, but she feels it. I feel it.

The library blinked its lights for closing, and rather than hide and huddle, Misty gathered her meager belongings and picked up one crane to carry home.

She cradled that folded paper as if it were an egg, a fragile piece of porcelain, a living being. She walked past all the shiny, rich, wooden tables, the chessmen, the stuffed animals of the Story Time playground.

She didn't see the librarians watch her with concern.

She didn't hear them call out.

Even though she'd walked through those doors daily for months, she forgot the last shallow step down leaving the lobby.

Then all I heard was screaming as the crane flew, airborne for a few seconds, into the night sky.

Misty crumbled down those steps.

But she never made a sound.

The scream was mine.

CHAPTER THIRTY-TWO

When Vivian, Leif, and George reached the library, the doors were closed and locked and the building seemed to sigh in slumber. *Or coma.*

"We can't leave," George implored. "She sleeps in there sometimes."

"In the library?"

Her brother nodded. "Yeah, she hides."

"How do you know?" Leif asked.

"I've watched her. Followed her." George shrugged. "She's really sick. I worried." My thoughts turned to Carlton.

"Can we get in?" Vivian tried a locked door.

"Breaking and entering?" Leif asked.

"If we have to." Vivian looked around and spotted boot soles. *A homeless person?* "I'll be right back."

She marched over toward the bushes. "Excuse me, I'm hoping you can help me find my friend. I'll be happy to buy you dinner in exchange?"

Several curious faces blinked out at her.

"I have sixty bucks. Twenty for each of you." Vivian reached into her bag and showed them cash. "My friend is very sick and we're trying to figure out if she's still in the library."

"They don't let people sleep in the library."

"I know," Vivian answered.

"Shame, it's big and warm."

"That's true," Vivian agreed.

"And dry."

"You looking for the girlie in the ambulance?"

Vivian perked up. "Ambulance?"

"Fell down the steps."

"Hauled her away."

"Never woke up. Looked like a junkie, if you ask me."

"She's sick." Leif held George's trembling shoulder in solidarity and support.

"Did this girl look anything like him?" Vivian pointed toward George.

"Could be. Dark and all. Hood over her hair, her face."

"The flashing lights hurt my eyes."

Leif edged closer. "How long ago did this happen?"

"Don't know. A hiccup of breaths."

"Thank you. Thank you for your help." Vivian handed the money over and ushered the boys back to the car.

Leif scowled. "That was dangerous."

Vivian didn't answer him.

Leif checked the time and swore. "I have to get to the airport to get Sam."

"Okay, split up. We'll go to the med center. It's closest, and if they see her scar they'll know she had a transplant. You want to come with me?" Vivian asked George.

"Yeah, I'm coming." The boy nodded vigorously.

Vivian touched Leif's hand. "Text me when you get Sam."

"And me if you find her."

There was an awkward moment when Leif bent to kiss Vivian and she went to hug him.

They were still angry and hurt and kind of strangers to each other.

Vivian ignored George's confused look and kissed Leif's cheek before grabbing George's hand and moving toward the main road.

"Hurry." She hailed a cab.

Yes, hurry.

CHAPTER THIRTY-THREE

Leif stood at the B concourse passenger exit amid the late-night gathering. Seeing each other via video conference didn't mean he and Samuel had officially met; Leif worried he somehow looked different in real life.

"Hey—" Samuel approached.

"Hey—" Leif responded with relief. Sam was shorter than he expected and appeared no older than thirteen.

Is that handshake–chest bump–half hug in boy DNA?

"We can't find Misty; Vivian went to the hospital." Leif brought Samuel up to speed on the way to the parking garage.

Samuel checked his phone and dropped a curse.

Leif glanced over at Samuel's agitation. "Wha?"

"My ma blew up my voice mail."

"She mad?"

"Beyond." Sam shrugged. "She's on her way. We gotta find Misty quick."

Thank god the voice mail filled up after thirty messages. Her shrill outrage makes my head hurt. Sam's gonna be in trouble.

Vivian texted her favorite nurse from the cab.

R U wkng?

"You know people here?" George asked as Vivian escorted him toward the main visitor entrance.

"I've spent a lot of time in this place."

Her phone beeped and she read the reply aloud. "'Y—you in ER? What happened?'"

Her fingers moving quickly, she responded. "I'm good. Friend might be here. Need help."

Almost immediately, the answer came: "Down in a sec."

Vivian felt better. "Nurse Heidi's going to come down. She knows everything that happens in this hospital."

"If they took her to the emergency room, shouldn't we be there?" George asked, studying the map of the medical center.

With its big windows and conversation areas upholstered in soothing blue (Pantone 277) and green (Pantone 12-0313), this was the least contaminated area of the waiting rooms. No one spent time here—they moved through to find patients and family. "Nurse Heidi will help us." Vivian had to be careful with her own health. The last thing she needed was exposure to a virus, or bacterial infection. She didn't want to say anything to Leif, or George, but while most people felt safe in hospitals, for her being in one could be deadly.

Big risk for a stranger.

Speaking from across the lobby, the nurse approached with a frown. "If you're not sick, you can't be here. Do you have any idea how dangerous this is?"

Vivian smiled. "Nice to see you too."

"No hugs—who the hell knows what's on these scrubs." It took a special person to wear teddy-bear scrubs and daisy antennae on a headband and scold with a grin on her face.

So this is Nurse Heidi of the Friday-night kettle corn, chocolate chip cookies, and ghost stories at two a.m.

"Extenuating circumstances," Vivian offered.

"They always are. What's going on?"

Down to business, Heidi listened to Vivian and George explain.

"I know it's against policy, but . . . ?" Vivian let her voice carry the rest of her question.

Privacy rules, patient confidentiality, perhaps the fact Misty never regained consciousness . . . We waited with held breath.

"If she's here, I'll find her," Heidi promised. "But you have to wait here, or better yet, outside, and then go home. And don't touch anything. You can't see her, Vivian. It's way too dangerous for you to be up on the floors."

"I know, but you can take George to her." Vivian gestured.

"I'll see what I can do."

"You're thirteen, right?" Heidi asked Misty's brother. *And I'm alive and you can see me. No one will believe that.*

Vivian answered for him. "Of course he is, no visitors can be younger than that."

George stayed silent.

Smart kid.

CHAPTER THIRTY-FOUR

I sat with Misty while they gently bathed her, bundled her in blankets, rehydrated her, and waited for test results.

Bodies are complicated. They sounded so simple in biology class. The systems were straightforward: circulatory, respiratory, digestive, and reproductive. There were more, but I didn't memorize them. With Vivian and Samuel part of my life, I knew about the endocrine and the lymph and metabolic. They, and so I, knew more than most med students hoped to cram inside their brains.

And yet there is nothing to do but sit with Misty.

How did all of those physical safeguards and redundant systems and parts fail? *Because there are a million ways the same piece can break.*

Samuel focused on cell memory and soul printing, though I knew his newfound love of sauerkraut had nothing to do with me and instead was merely the process of living life. Exploring. Tasting. Trying. Loving. Failing.

Epic failing.

Misty's skin was bloated and rashy, tinged with gray and yellow, like an old bruise.

I felt her snipping the threads connecting her soul to her body. *She's getting ready to fly. Why can't I fly?*

I felt Samuel's anxiety and questions pounding closer to the hospital.

There are a thousand million little miracles that when done right make a human being live. And yet none of these turn a living body into a life worthwhile. Lives are lived beyond the numbers. In the space between the miracles.

I didn't fly away because I was waiting. Waiting for something I couldn't name, something I'd know when I saw it, and only then.

When Nurse Heidi escorted George to Misty's hospital bed, Vivian did as promised and left the hospital. She headed for the studio.

She needed her paints. Her colors. The soothing of vibrants, not pastels. The splashes of fuchsia and violets of sunrises. The vast expanse of endless nights with full blue moons.

She needed the smell of wood frames and treated canvas and fresh paint.

The feel of color sliding over itself and mixing.

Some people needed chocolate or macaroni and cheese to soothe; Viv needed color.

Misty wasn't going to live. Vivian knew enough that not even a single cell in her held out hope for a miracle or a redo. Misty had been lucky to get a second chance; she wouldn't get a third.

How many times had Vivian faced this hopeless feeling?

She wanted control; she wanted predictability. She wanted the impossible. She wanted life served up on a canvas with straight edges and perfect corners, the mess elegant and defined, beauty evident in at least a square inch of the space.

There was nothing beautiful about dying. Misty's body shutting down was ugly.

Dying is ugly.

Vivian mixed blues and reds for the deep purples, but they kept going brown.

She scraped and started again.

Brown.

Ugly.

Dying.

Out of control.

Out of her control.

Vivian scraped the canvas again. Each stroke angrier, rougher, more impatient.

With each exhale she shoved paint around the canvas and another face flashed in her mind's eye.

Sally.

Blob the paint onto the canvas.

Brian.

Blow it north.

Wallace.

Brush it south.

Crystal.

Another splash of blue from the west.

Billy.

Blow it southeast.

Misty.

Me.

Blue and red bled into each other until brown became black at the center.

Vivian collapsed with her head in her hands and cried.

When Leif and he arrived at the hospital, Samuel tucked the worry dolls and prayer beads into his cargo pants pocket. They asked for Nurse Heidi as Vivian instructed.

"Where's Vivian?" Leif glanced around, expecting to see her waiting.

"Dude, she can't be here. It's too dangerous," Samuel answered in a loud and surprised voice.

"How do you know that?" Nurse Heidi asked as she approached.

"I know about transplants." Sam didn't offer his own experience as evidence, and when Leif opened his mouth, Sam's icy glare shut him up. *Yeah, you shouldn't be here either, genius.*

George shook Samuel's hand with an adultlike expression that belied his eleven years. He was almost the same height and outweighed Sam by a good thirty pounds. "You're her friend, right? Who she talks to online?"

"Yeah." Samuel didn't notice that he was the smallest person there.

"Thanks. You helped her."

"How?" Sam's expression was full of total bewilderment. They were standing in a hospital, for heaven's sake. How helpful was he?

George shrugged. "She seemed happier talking to you."

"He followed her to the library a lot, keeping an eye on her," the nurse said, and introduced herself.

"She told me she was taking the medicine. That she went to her doctor. She lied," George whispered.

"Hey. This is not your fault," Samuel reassured George.

"Then whose is it?" George asked no one in particular.

"George, we need to call your parents." The nurse stopped them at the door to the room.

"How bad is it?" Leif asked the question no one else seemed willing to voice.

"We're waiting for test results, and I can only tell her parents what the results of those are."

He knew that. He wasn't sure why he bothered to ask.

She paused and seemed to understand they needed more than that. "She is not in pain. She's comfortable."

Samuel nodded.

"But if you have anything you want to say, you should say it sooner rather than later." She held George's shoulders in a motherly hug and led him toward the main counter. The boy cried silently, tears rolling straight down his cheeks, as if there were permanent tracks for them to follow. They all knew what she meant.

That was it. That was all Sam needed to hear.

Leif put his hand on Samuel's shoulder. Briefly. Gently.

"You should go find Vivian," Samuel said without turning around.

"I can go in with you, if you want—" Leif crossed his arms.

"No, man, I'm gonna stay till they kick me out."

Leif didn't know how to help but he needed to do something. "Are you hungry? I can grab food and bring it back."

"Sure, but take your time."

Sam mentally recited the thirteenth Psalm as he turned the knob and pushed open the oversize door. A chorus of beeps and blips and hisses were shrouded in darkness.

He swallowed hard, then dragged a chair next to Misty's bedside.

Her eyes were closed, almost swollen shut, her face round and peaceful. Her belly puffed up the covers oddly. Sam knew that was the organ failure; her liver wasn't doing its job anymore. He picked up her hand and cradled it gently. Her fingers were smudged with black, as if she'd been handling a lot of newsprint, or copies with mucked-up ink.

Samuel closed his eyes, rested his forehead on her hand, and began to speak.

"Dear Lord, Yahweh, Jehovah, Messiah, the unnamed power of the universe. Your people call you many names, they praise you in many languages, they ask you for many gifts. You have granted me many miracles and have been present in my life in many ways. Misty needs you now. Please be with her. Hold her hand and keep her safe. Aid her sleep, bring her peace, and if it's time, please take her home. Let her live or make her die, but no more slow suffering. It's too much to bear."

Across the bed, I held Misty's other hand. And when Sam said "Amen," I echoed him and we waited.

CHAPTER THIRTY-FIVE

Leif lifted a couple of fingers when Vivian glanced toward the window. He loved watching her work. The expression on her face seemed as though she saw beyond this world into another, more beautiful, more expressive world.

She opened the door and stepped back. "So?"

"The nurse pretty much told us she's dying. I came to see if you're okay."

"Of course I'm okay."

"You took a big risk going to the hospital, didn't you?"

Vivian shrugged. "I should have stayed."

"Uh, no." Leif's breath caught, thinking about Vivian being in that bed, dying instead.

"She shouldn't have been alone."

"According to Sam, we're never alone."

"God? You believe that?"

"Maybe. I don't disbelieve."

She nodded. "I'm sorry for fighting with you."

"Me too. I don't even know what I did."

"It's not important." She shook her head. "You've been a good friend."

Leif blanched and felt a pulse of shock hit his heart. "Just friends?"

Vivian turned away and began tidying up.

She's nervous. Lying. Does he know her well enough to see it?

"Of course we're friends," she answered, not making eye contact.

"That's all I am to you?"

"What else is there for us?"

"What else?" Leif growled. "You get me. You fill empty spaces inside I didn't know I had. I love you."

The shock on Vivian's face quickly dissipated behind disbelief and fear. If she believed him, if she went there, there was no going back. "I have a mustache." She narrowed her eyes with the admission as if waiting for him to run.

He shrugged. "I can't grow one."

She crossed her arms. "My gums are swallowing my teeth."

"They'll cut them off before you're toothless." He stepped forward.

"My face is the shape of an undercooked pancake. I have no cheekbones."

He stepped forward until he was almost within touching distance. "Oh, come on, you make yourself sound like Quasimodo."

Her eyes widened, and she nodded as if he finally understood her. "Exactly. Are you sure they didn't hit your head?"

He reached for her. "Puhleez. You're being dramatic. My grandmother has a mustache."

"I'm like your grandmother?" Vivian blanched.

"Yes. Well, I love her, but I don't want to have sex with her, so no. You're not. Maybe. Dammit, Vivian, I don't even know what's going on here." He shoved forward until they almost touched.

She huffed.

"Viv, look at me." He lifted his hands to cup her shoulders and then dropped them without following through.

No, touch her! Touch her!

"Don't make fun of me." She sniffled, near tears.

"I'm not. I'm really not. I just don't know what to say. You don't believe me."

"What?" She flipped around as if that was the last thing she expected him to say.

"I tell you I think you're beautiful and you don't believe me. What else can I say? You may have a new heart and lungs, but you need glasses."

"Oh, now I need glasses?"

"Look. I get it. I'm supposed to be in love with the head cheerleader with her perfect hair and that face of makeup and her fake 'n' bake tan. But she eats saltines and drinks water at lunch. You eat a triple cheeseburger with smothered fries and wash it down with a chocolate shake. You laugh at my jokes and tell me I have a good singing voice. You talk about real life, not reality-television princesses."

She wrinkled her nose. "You do have a good voice—"

"I'm not going on tour anytime soon and we both know it, but you look at me and you don't see a future gold medal or a hundred-million-dollar contract offer."

"If you wanted those, I would support you—"

"I know you would. I really know it in my gut. That's why I

253

love you. Tell me this, why do you have a mustache and a round face and lots of gums?"

"Because of the meds," she answered, dropping her eyes.

Leif knelt to keep eye contact, and when he winced, she pushed him into a chair. "And without the meds?"

"I would reject the organs and the CF would take over other stuff."

He clasped her hands. "And without a heart or lungs? With the CF winning?"

"What do you mean?"

"If you didn't have a working heart, or a set of lungs that moved air, what would happen to you?"

She frowned and squinted at him like he'd lost his mind, but I saw where he was headed and I liked it. *Go, Leif!* Never in a million years did I think I'd ever cheer on a baller.

"I'd be dead," she finally answered in a tiny voice.

"Uh-huh. So . . ." Leif's voice boomed like he'd won the game. "So?"

"So you're here. With me. Living. That's beautiful to me. You make me want to do more than go through the motions."

She nodded.

"Besides, I can teach you to shave."

They cracked up and she snorted snot through her tears.

"You're alive, Viv. That's sexy to me. That's a gift." He hugged her.

She laid her head on his shoulder and melted into his strength. "I love you too."

CHAPTER THIRTY-SIX

Samuel, George, and I kept vigil into the night. The nurses were having a hard time finding Misty's parents, but they kept trying.

"She's going to die, isn't she?" George asked Sam.

Samuel hadn't stopped praying, but he felt sure there were no miracles left to be had. "I think so."

George nodded.

"Please, God, let her see my face before she leaves. Let her look upon someone who loves her. Let her see her brother here with her." Samuel kept repeating this plea over and over in his head. He screamed it so loudly, internally, I was sure everyone, not just me, heard it.

At some point, the younger boy fell asleep with his head on the bed. Sam covered him with a blanket and sat back down.

Quietly, and with tenderness, Samuel's ma touched his shoulder. "Samuel, she's not going to wake up, honey. But she doesn't hurt anymore either."

Samuel grabbed his ma's hand. He held on so tightly I worried her bones might snap. Her expression told me she'd do anything to take this pain from her son. How horrible must it be for parents to say good-bye, or to watch their children suffer?

How are my own parents, my brother, handling my death?

Samuel wiped his nose and rubbed his eyes with the heels of his hands.

Mrs. Sabir waited in silence, then with a deep breath said, "Honey, it's not safe for you to be in the hospital. What about infection?"

Leave him alone.

"Sam, she's not going to wake up. We need to get you away from the germs."

He shook off his ma's touch. "Leave if you want. I am staying."

I witnessed the confusion on her face, the fear that he was defying her again. To need her comfort so desperately one second and shake her off the next was life in the microcosm. She didn't know how to handle this swift change. She looked so lost, and so ambushed by his adulthood, I almost felt sorry for her. With a nod, she slunk out into the hall without saying anything.

Samuel didn't notice. His hands cradled Misty's and he returned to his prayerful plea.

CHAPTER THIRTY-SEVEN

Leif grabbed three kinds of burgers, enough fries to feed a defensive line, and sodas.

"You're not coming in. You promised," he demanded.

"I promise, but you'll text me. If anything happens. Anything changes."

"Of course."

"But don't let anyone see your phone. Technically, they're supposed to be off, but we all sneak them."

"Okay."

"And ask Heidi who's on shift after her and I'll tell you who to talk to."

"Okay."

"And—"

Leif interrupted. "Vivian, the food is getting icy."

"Sorry."

"I'll be with Sam and I will bring him to your house if he'll let me."

"And if his mom is here—"

"She can come too. I heard your mom say she'd get the guest rooms ready."

Vivian kissed him quickly, almost embarrassed by the new intimacy. "Thank you."

Leif tossed his jacket over the food and hurried down the hallway toward Misty's room.

He stopped when he saw George and Samuel out in the hallway. "What's going on?"

"Shift change. The doctor is checking her; we need to wait outside."

"It's normal." Sam's mom patted Leif's arm. "Sit down."

"I brought food."

"Good, the boys are hungry. Here, George, you have to eat." She immediately took over mothering. George seemed to appreciate the attention.

The doctor and Nurse Heidi stepped out. I stayed where I was at Misty's side.

"We need to find your parents," Heidi repeated to George.

"Are you her guardian?" the doctor asked Samuel's mom.

She shook her head. "I'm sorry, I don't know how to reach them."

"The number of visitors is usually limited to two at a time. But until we locate the rest of her family—"

"Thank you," Samuel answered.

"Doctor, will you please instruct my son to—"

"Ma. Not now." The strength in Sam's tone sounded anything but childlike and everything adult. "Please."

"Yes?" The doctor checked the chart, but paused.

"—eat his dinner. Tell him to keep his strength up."

"What she said." The doctor pointed at Sam's mom and gave a small smile. "Once a mom, always a mom."

As he walked away, Leif leaned toward Sam and said, "If Vivian shouldn't be here, you shouldn't either, right? It's risky for you."

"I can't leave."

"Mrs. Sabir, Vivian's family has prepared a guest room for you that you're welcome to use," Leif said. "I can take you over there if you'd like."

"That's so kind, but I don't know—"

"Give us a minute, okay?" Sam asked Leif.

"Sure." Leif ushered George into Misty's room.

"Ma, I have to stay. I need to see this through—"

"But, Samuel, if you get an infection—"

"Then I get an infection. Ma, Misty has the same donor as me. We met on the Internet. God brought us together for a reason."

"That reason isn't for you to both die."

"Ma," Samuel said, exasperated. "You wanted me to be well so I could have a life, right? Have a future? Fall in love? Go to Paris? Be a man?"

"Yes, but—"

"I'm being a man and doing the right thing, the hardest thing, and being here for my friend when she dies."

"I see."

"I have to do this on my own."

"But—"

"Go home, Ma. Please. I'll be back in a few days."

The sadness in her face broke Samuel's heart. He had to break away; he needed to stand on his own and not need her so much. He wasn't sick anymore.

He tried to soften the divide. "I really appreciate how much you've taken care of me. You're a wonderful mother. And I'm grateful that you never let me stop hoping that I could survive and get well. But I'm not sick anymore, and I'm seventeen, almost eighteen. I need to stay here. And find out about my donor."

"Will you keep your cell phone with you? And you'll answer when I call or text? You won't leave me hanging?"

"I promise."

"And you'll let me know where you're going and who you're with and—"

"I promise, Ma. I'll crash with Leif, or in Vivian's guest room. They're good people. Vivian's an artist—you'd recognize her work. Leif's parents are famous athletes. Nothing bad is going to happen."

"Don't say that, Samuel. You don't test God's patience with jokes like that."

"You're right. But nothing bad is going to happen to me because of my friends."

"You will leave the hospital at the first opportunity, and you will be careful and take all your medications and avoid grapefruit, and if you feel the slightest bit ill, you will see a doctor immediately?"

"I promise. I promise all of that. Now I need to go sit with Misty."

"Eat the food."

"Yes, ma'am."

"I'm going home. I'll catch a flight in the morning. But I can stay in a hotel and just be here if you need me? You know you always can call your father's family. They live around here somewhere."

"Yes, Ma. I have Aunt Rita's address."

"Okay, then."

"I need you, Ma. I'll always need you, but you don't need to stay."

"Are you sure?"

"Yes, yes, now go."

Misty's closet-size room was crowded with three boys impatiently waiting for something, anything, to happen.

The stillness got to them all.

"I'm going to the bathroom. Want a pop?" George asked the others.

"I'll come with you." Leif stretched his legs. "Want anything?"

Sam shook his head. What he wanted wasn't in a vending machine.

I'd love a Diet Coke.

Samuel and I were left alone with Misty. When she stirred, we both thought we were imagining things. But when she blinked and opened her eyes, we all held our breath.

"Misty? It's Sam." Samuel wanted to hear her voice. He wanted her to sit up, stand, and walk out of there as if the entire thing were just a simple misunderstanding. "Hi."

Misty blinked. Her eyelids fluttered closed, then opened again.

Sam touched her cheek. "Do you hurt anywhere? I can call the nurse."

Misty didn't move, but she wasn't in pain.

I felt her surprise that he was there, but even more, I felt the jolt when she recognized me.

She sees me.

I felt her hand squeeze mine and I squeezed back.

She tilted her head back toward Samuel, wanting to tell him I was there too.

"I prayed you'd wake up to know you're not alone. George will be back any minute. And they're trying to find your parents."

Misty tried to speak, but the words evaporated long before they made it to her tongue.

"I'll stay here as long as I need to. You are going to be okay. No more slow suffering."

Misty managed to nod.

Samuel wanted to reassure her that God was there, that she was going to a better place, but his faith faltered. What if he promised her things that weren't true?

I'm here.

On reflex, I reached out and touched his head, completing the circle with Misty between us.

His voice strengthened and deepened with assurance and belief. "You'll be better than okay. You're not alone."

Misty turned to look at me and for a moment I think Sam saw me too, and then we both faded.

CHAPTER THIRTY-EIGHT

The best way to describe my reality was to say that I was in multiple places at once. There. Here. Paris. Iowa. The grocery store on Sixth and Lexington. Wherever my living pieces went, I went. But I could also choose to go beyond. Misty moved on. For everyone else, that meant she died. For me, that just meant onward. Some things words never adequately expressed.

George led the way behind the chessmen and around the tables. No one paid our group any attention. Samuel, Leif, Vivian, George, and me.

"It's up those stairs." George pointed.

Leif saw the kid's stony expression. "You're not coming."

George shook his head. It wasn't as if anyone blamed him. I wouldn't go either.

Vivian hugged George's bony shoulders and then marched up the stairs. "Wow."

They saw the crane collection for the first time, like a flock was passing through, stopping to rest overnight. Cranes of all sizes, made out of candy wrappers and garbage, notebook paper and class worksheets, rested on every available inch of space. A librarian followed us up, but Leif's quiet conversation charmed her into retreat. I wondered how long we had before Misty's cranes migrated to the Dumpster.

"I still don't understand why they're not burying her and having a funeral," Samuel groused.

"Cremation is their custom, and they want her sent back to their hometown," Vivian answered. Again.

"I don't think they can afford it." Leif shrugged.

"She's American; she belongs here." Samuel seemed surprised at his own vehemence, and then added, almost silently, "With us."

"She's dead. She belongs anywhere she wants to be," Vivian gently reminded us all.

They lapsed into contemplation. There was something magical in that tiny space of birds and souls.

Leif was the first to see the binder tucked under the computer station and read Samuel's name on the letter.

Samuel read the note, tucked the thick stack of bills into his pack. He ran his fingers over the keyboard and sat in Misty's chair. "Let's go," he said.

They all picked a crane; Vivian took an extra for George.

"You sure about this?" Leif asked again.

"We have to," Samuel answered, with a determined nod from Vivian.

He's not going to let us in. No way was Mother home. He might not even open the door. I always fielded visitors. I protected him. *Now he has to protect himself.*

"You must be Carlton?" Vivian asked.

That's my baby brother.

The three of them stood on the porch of my mother's condo. I hadn't been back since leaving for the party. Lifetimes ago.

"Who are you?" he asked, narrowing his eyes.

"We kinda know your sister."

In an almost biblical way, if Leif and Vivian have their way. Thanks, Samuel, for giving me religious knowledge. Too bad I can't be on a game show.

Vivian held out a copy of my obituary as if this was all the evidence he should need. I brushed past the open door as far as I could go into the house. I tried to hug Carlton, touch him, reassure him. But he didn't seem to feel me.

"Oh, cool." Carlton's grip on the door handle loosened, and I heard him give a gentle sigh. I think he misses me as much as I've missed him. I watched myriad emotions flit over his face. *He wants to let them in. He wants to know about my pieces. He's not weirded out at all.*

Vivian asked, "We were hoping we can talk to your mom? We'd like to say hello."

"Did you get her organs?" Carlton queried.

Leave it to Carlton to cut right to the heart of it all.

"Yes, I have her heart and lungs."

Samuel offered, "I have her kidneys and pancreas."

Carlton turned to Leif. "And you?"

"Soft tissue and bone to rebuild my leg."

"Can I see the scars? Can you talk to her? Is she in heaven?" As if no one had spoken to him since the hospital to answer his questions, the floodgates opened, and Carlton wouldn't stop talking.

"Um, s-sure," Vivian stuttered.

"Come on in." He opened the door and invited them all inside. "Mother isn't here, but she should be home soon. Wanna see Jess's room?"

My bedroom?

The house looked exactly the same. Beige and gray and neutrals on every surface. The light scent of vanilla room freshener lingered. It felt sterile and empty.

"Please."

My bedroom furniture matched, whitewashed wood from my mother's shabby-chic phase. Nothing had changed except the dirty laundry that was missing from the hamper and the floor.

They stood there as if being in my bedroom might help them understand me better. Know me even a little bit. *I'm not that same girl.*

My life was beige. Not beige in a bad way. But I'd learned that other people roar through the world in fuchsia, or neon orange, or even determined black. But me, I was off-white or ecru. Given another chance, I might sprinkle in spring green or wash in waves of Mediterranean Sea teals. Add the heat of roaring red peppers, or voluptuous violet sensuality. I would work in a little lemon-yellow tart, both sweet and fresh. Jessica Chai was beige, but now? Pieces of me are anything but beige.

My heart is midnight blue.

My lungs a mossy green and chocolate brown.

My eyes a clear, unfettered gray.

My kidneys rich cranberry and my bones a strong ivory.

The real me wasn't in this house, wasn't in that bland and mediocre world where this teen trio all waited for a clue, a revelation, an answer.

Carlton disappeared and returned holding Mr. Peepers, a stuffed bunny I slept with every night until sixth grade. "Here."

Vivian reached out to take the worn bunny from Carlton's outstretched hands. "Who's this?" She assumed correctly that there was a name attached.

"Her bunny. I kept it."

He doesn't know Mr. Peepers's name?

"Nice to meet you, bunny." Vivian made eye contact with the stuffed animal, then gently handed him back to Carlton.

"Mother is turning this into a guest room."

"So your mom has taken Jessica's things out of here?" Samuel asked, as if the emptiness of the room could be explained away.

And I realized then that my bedroom had also changed. My clothes were gone from the closet. The computer on the desk had been replaced by a dried- and silk-flower arrangement.

Carlton nodded. "I kept this. Don't tell Mother."

"We won't."

"Hello?"

I heard the click of heels downstairs and my mother's voice call the question up. That one word crashed the distance, and time, and all of the change, into me. The impact left me as breathless, and broken, as the accident itself. I crumpled to the floor and watched with only half an eye.

Carlton said, "They have Jessica."

Vivian, Samuel, and Leif greeted my mother with deference and respect. "We are recipients."

Mother acted as though she'd anticipated their visit and invited them, "Of course. We'll have tea." She hesitated. "Downstairs. If you'll come this way," she commanded, and closed the bedroom door behind them. I wanted to stay there, but the ribbon connecting us dragged me to the stairs. I missed the beginning of the conversation. I lost time. Perspective.

They all held teacups and saucers. The plate of bakery cookies and quickly thawed pound cake sat untouched.

My mother studied Vivian from the corner of her eye, as if trying to catch a glimpse of my face.

"The hardest part was watching them wheel her away," my mother muttered in answer to a question I didn't catch. "Tell me about you." She turned on the charm and deflected talking about me time and again.

She never knew me.

CHAPTER THIRTY-NINE

Samuel crawled off to bed sometime after midnight, leaving Leif and Vivian cuddling in her rec room. None of them, of us, really wanted the day to end.

"This is it?" Vivian traced her fingers over Leif's scars. Tiny pink ones (Pantone 7590 and 17-1524) and larger, meatier keloid scars that told her there was a lot of reconstruction along his limb (Pantone 18-1248).

"Yeah, the rebuilt knee. Parts bionic. Parts Jessica." Leif stretched as if to prove he still held dominion over the leg.

Vivian's fingertips whispered sympathies. "Looks painful."

"It was, but it's better every day."

She laughed. "Liar."

He shrugged. "Okay, but it will be fine soon."

"Hmm." Vivian laid her cheek against his chest and they reveled in the touch. This was life. Living.

I felt Leif lick his lips and work up courage. "Vivian, can I see it?"

"I told you, not until it's finished," she mumbled.

"I meant your scar."

Vivian sat up and tilted her head in question. "Why?"

"I'm curious."

In any other case, Vivian knew she'd feel like a circus act, freak-show entertainment, but Leif wasn't asking in that way.

She started to pull her shirt up. "You'll have to help me, or I'll flash you."

"Well . . ." Leif leaned away. "Maybe I can't help, then."

She rolled her eyes. "It traces under my boobs around the back there." With her hands securely on her breasts, he gently crinkled up the thermal henley and then her camisole.

Vivian was used to all sorts of strangers seeing her naked. It wasn't that she was modest—being a patient at a teaching hospital her whole life forfeited the desire to have clothing covering skin. But Leif's gaze was different. He wasn't looking at her like a case, a patient; he was looking at her like a boy studies a girl.

Golden goose bumps rose on her arms and back (Pantone 100). She shivered.

Leif froze. "Want me to stop?"

"No. It's okay."

He nodded and went back to studying her body. Smaller scars from chest tubes and biopsies and procedures crisscrossed her stomach and chest like a topographical map. Her body marked time in scar tissue and sutures.

I sat with my back to them, needing their closeness, needing to witness, but wanting to provide privacy.

After a few minutes, the silence tortured Vivian. Did he find her ugly? Broken? Unworthy? "Say something."

"It's not bad." Leif didn't glance up, didn't understand the gravity of her demand.

Vivian deflated slightly. "Expecting something Frankensteinish?"

"Maybe. I don't know." He reached out the tip of his finger to trace the line. "Does it hurt?"

"Not the scar. Not anymore."

"What hurts, then?"

"Making plans."

"What?" Leif dropped her shirt and sat up to study her face.

"You were right. It's hard to want more, because I should be content with simply still being here."

"Because of all the death, you mean?"

"They're not here, and a bad day for me would still be more time here for them. It feels wrong to be greedy."

"Oh, Viv—"

"Wait, let me finish. It felt wrong. But that's changed. I don't know why—maybe it was finally seeing Jessica's life and meeting her brother—but if I can't make plans for me, I have to do it for her."

"But we only saw her house, not her life."

"Isn't it the same?" Vivian hunkered into her assumption with a frown.

Um, no! No, it's not the same thing.

"Is it?"

"Then why did we go? If not to know her?"

"The house she lived in is only one piece of her. Just like the heart is only one piece of you."

"You're right. All the more reason to look ahead, right?"

Leif nodded. "Sure."

"I'll probably backslide."

"I'll catch you."

"Thanks." Vivian leaned over and kissed Leif gently.
Thank you.

CHAPTER FORTY

Samuel logged on to The-Daily-Miracle first. With a quick cut-and-paste, he uploaded his latest blog post.

Dear Miracle Watchers,
    I started this blog as a way to reach out to all the people seeking hope. No, that's a lie. I started this blog because I needed to see hope at work. I needed it. You see, I've spent years of my life on dialysis, waiting for my own miracle of an organ transplant. My faith that all things happen for a reason was tested repeatedly. The blog made me feel as if I had a reason to be here.
    I am not going to quote statistics, but honestly, at the heart of the matter, I didn't think I would ever get kidneys. Thanks to a family in another state and a girl named Jessica, I did.
    That was the miracle I expected. Prayed for. Needed. But the true miracle was meeting the other people who are now connected to me via Jessica. Yes, all things happen for a reason.

And I fell in love.

There I said it. Typed it too. I fell in love with a girl I'd never met; we seemed to connect better than anyone else on the entire planet. I know it sounds impossible, but I've already posted thousands of impossible things over the years. Don't tell me that falling in love with someone you've never met seems the most impossible of all.

You don't have to believe me. The love was real, and I will always love her.

But she isn't here anymore, and I can't be with her. I can't explain, but I know that she and Jessica are together.

My gift to her, to both of them, is to live for us all.

I need to live.

A new friend brought to my attention that I am no longer tethered to tubes and hospitals every day for hours. Scary as stepping into the unknown is, I also need to step away from the computer wires and screens. A wise man told me I'm not actually living if I don't go out and get dirty.

"You gotta get tackled and muddy. Computers aren't life," he said.

I can't say the tackling appeals, but perhaps that's an inevitable part of playing this game of life. Sometimes we get tackled. And some of us can't get up. And others require help but can bounce back. What can I say? The computer geek likes sports metaphors too.

So I'm taking a break from the blog. I've opened the links to all of us. I ask that you please share miracles as you spot them. Make miracles of your own happen for others.

I'll be honest: I'm terrified. But I've learned we are all connected to each other. I have friends all around the world, and I'm counting on you. I guess that's what I wanted to show all along.

Enough. For now. I'll upload virtual postcards if the mood strikes and check in from time to time. I'll be back. But in the meantime, I might see you at the La Brea Tar Pits in Los Angeles or New York's Dylan's Candy Bar, the pyramids at Giza or Bangkok's newest nightclub.

I don't know exactly where, but I'll be living outside the box where all the dirty mess lives. Watch for me and say hello.

ONE-YEAR ANNIVERSARY

CHAPTER FORTY-ONE

At what point I knew everything about their lives I don't know. One moment I was me and the next I was more than, like flipping through cable channels on an out-of-this-world remote. There was more to my story than just me.

Living takes something else. Something greater. Something more. The miracles that made my body work did not give me the sight, the heart, the ear for life. My life mattered, but not in the living, in the dying. My life made the continuation of these lives possible.

"You're sure this is the right place?"

"Carlton printed directions."

I'd never been in this cemetery, never seen my own grave. Maybe I never wanted to.

"We have to work fast. They shut the gates and patrol on Halloween night."

"You think they might wonder why we have shovels?" Samuel chuckled.

Maybe.

Vivian unwrapped the four-by-four canvas.

Her work stole my breath.

Me.

Them.

Beautiful.

Leif and Samuel grinned and began to carefully peel the sod from my grave. "You're sure we have to bury this for her?"

"Can't we just leave it by her headstone?"

"You heard them say that they remove everything on the first of the month. I don't want this ending up in the Dumpster or on a collector's wall."

"Why can't we keep it?" Leif asked.

"I'm painting special ones for all of us," Vivian answered. "Dig."

My face was there, smiling as if I knew a special secret. My hair was short like in the photo Mother showed them from dress shopping. But Vivian painted me full of tiny adventures. Up close I saw birthday cakes with candles, hubcaps, baby rattles, running shoes, flags of Great Britain and Kenya and Malaysia. Wedding rings and white doves. Forks and a T-bone steak. The Parthenon and the Grand Canyon's walls. Every time I saw it, studied it, there was something else, something new.

Like life.

As if the painting evolved as their journeys unfolded. With new textures and perspectives. New colors and depths.

The boys moved dirt onto the tarp, just a few inches, deep enough to cover the portrait from groundskeepers and prying eyes.

Vivian laid it gently down and silently they filled the dirt on top, positioned the grass exactly the way it was.

I'm attending my own funeral.

Samuel popped sodas and they plunked down, leaning against gravestones. "How's Maestro George doing?" he asked Leif.

Leif's weekly piano lessons from the Maestro had started out as a way to keep in touch with Misty's brother but quickly morphed into a Leolin project. "He loves my parents. They're talking Carnegie Hall and Juilliard. He pretty much lives with us now since his parents are divorcing. They checked out after Misty's death, man."

"Is George cool with your parents being so on top of him?"

"Yeah, he doesn't mind the pressure, and they're beginning to think my love of music isn't so loserish. He lives for your post-cards and letters—calls you the Answer Man and won't tell me what you talk about."

"You got the recording of his recital?"

"Yeah, amazing. How's Carlton?"

"He and George are BFFs, and he spends almost as much time with us as George does. But you know his mom; she's all about tweeting photos of her with my parents. Poor kid."

Vivian twined her fingers with Leif's. "Carlton actually likes to paint, so I've got him in the store a couple days a week after school."

"He still likes to listen to your heart?"

"Yeah. Sometimes, when he's really sad, he holds up the stethoscope we got him and takes a listen."

They slid into gentle silence and watched flocks of birds heading south for winter. "Where are you off to next?" Vivian asked Samuel.

"There is a monastery in the mountains of Tibet that invited me to visit."

"And your mom?"

"She's taken up riding motorcycles and started a support group for parents of donors," Sam replied.

"How about you?"

Vivian answered, "I get my GED results next week, and then I start a course of study at the Sorbonne."

"Your parents let go of high school graduation?"

"We compromised." They finally understood that expecting Vivian's life to follow the normal journey didn't mean it would. They couldn't will it, just like they couldn't will a cure for her CF.

I think I always expected my life to start when I was an adult. After high school. After prom. After. After. After. I didn't think about trying to make every breath count, or whether or not my body might fail. My life did start after, but I was just along for the ride.

"What about you?" Samuel asked Leif.

"I'm training for a triathlon with Pirate. I missed working out and competition."

"You going to end up a pro player anyway?"

"Never. It's gotta stay fun or it's not worth it. There's more to my life than w's and l's." Leif draped his arm over the cool stone with my name chiseled into it and I thought about the days since my death.

I didn't know if my parents would have donated my organs if my hair had not been cut. If things were different, I knew they'd have leapt at the chance to keep me alive and accept anyone's organ if it was offered to save my life.

The funny part, ironic maybe—I had no idea who ended up with my hair. The ponytail that started this whole chain was missing in action. Maybe because the hair cells were already dead, or because I was still living when it was cut off my head, I had no energetic connection. I didn't know. Did a little girl somewhere wash and comb and wear my hair? Did she think of me the way Vivian did? Or Sam? Or Leif? Or did my hair even end up at the right place? Was it tossed in the trash like the garbage?

How did one death change the path of a life? Of many lives?

We'll see, won't we?

Everyone wants their life to count. In every heartbeat and breath, in steps, and sights, in touches and songs written—this is how I count mine.

"Next year we'll skydive," Samuel declared.

Vivian nodded. "Something new every anniversary of the rest of our lives?"

"I'm in," Leif agreed.

"We'll keep in touch?

"One of us, preferably all of us, needs to be here on the first of every 'more' year," Samuel commanded.

"On All Souls'? That's fitting."

"I don't like to think this is the only place she is." Vivian wiped away a stray tear.

Samuel's voice strengthened. "No matter what, on this day we'll report to Jessica on the mores in our lives. And Misty."

"The mores?" Leif asked.

Vivian got it. "More breaths."

"More birthdays," Sam added.

Leif smiled. "More kisses."

"More giggles."

"More shits." Samuel grinned.

"More chili dogs."

"More pets."

"More sex."

"More sleeping in."

"More staying up all night."

"More coffee."

"More speeding."

"More leaping."

"More running."

"More lazy yellow afternoons."

"More everything!" Vivian waved her hands at the sky, shouting.

Samuel leapt up and joined her, yelling, "And anything!"

"And all of it!" Leif roared so loud all of heaven heard.

There were mores because of me.

And just as I knew everything about these people, I knew they would keep their promises. They'd live, and gather, and share with me, if only in the back of their minds, what a full life we'd have. *Will I continue to journey with them? Or is there a "more" for me, waiting for me to be ready for it?*

I didn't know exactly when it happened, but there it was . . . the sum of my pieces was my peace.

Acknowledgments

I owe a debt of gratitude to those who have shared their amazing stories, including Reg Green, author of *The Nicholas Effect*, and Chris Klug, coauthor of *To the Edge and Back*. During the revision process I stumbled across Laura Rothenberg's memoir, *Breathing for a Living*, which documents her struggles with cystic fibrosis and ultimately her decision to undergo a double lung transplant. Afterward, I learned she died the same year her book was released. I owe her and her honest words: not only did her story help me better understand a teenage transplant patient's reality and color Vivian's life, but she also documents a girl who fought CF to have a life on her own terms. I hope Laura would approve of Vivian's spirit.

The Internet can be a wonderful place to find resources and stories, and I have to thank all the people who willingly and openly share their struggles with failing health, organ donations, survivors, and medical personnel via blogs, posts, and interviews. Thank you all for sharing with strangers your point of view.

I couldn't do what I do without the support of family and friends. Mary and Jeff Bakeman; Misty and Donnie Bittinger; Rosie, Tom, Elizabeth, and Aidan Donnelly; Sarah Diers; Patrick Boin; Sarri Gilman; Mark and Kate LaMar; Sarah and Tim LaMar; Lindsay Lanson; Barbara Lanzer; Tara Kelly; Pete Kizer; Rachel and Ken Rogers; Trudi and Bill Trueit; Barney and Beth Wick; Keith and Alyssa Wick; Kathy Wick; Mark Wick; Heidi Rendall; Erika and Scott Jones; Bruce Alexander; and Gail LaForest.

Booksellers like Tracy Harrison, Josh Hauser, and Nancy Welles, who hand-sell their favorite stories to new readers, are priceless. Many thanks for all you do.

Thank you to all the educators who hand-deliver stories to their students in a time when reading is being shoved aside for standardized tests. Our generations of thinkers and curiosity seekers are in your hands—please stay strong and fight for the love of learning.

Thanks to my beta readers who willingly wander into the lion's den of my head: Kate LaMar, Jennifer Sand, Tristan Wisont, Kim Mattingly, Meagan Parker, Danielle Mitchell, and Rachel Rogers.

To Mom, who never knew she cared so much about hearing tales of organ donation and cystic fibrosis—thank you for understanding my process and believing in serendipity too. To Alex, who has survived his first book with me and finally worked up the courage to ask, "When do you know a book is done, exactly?" Honey, I do so love you.

I always acknowledge our men and women in the military, naming some of the deployed while I am working on a book. It keeps me grounded and puts my process in perspective. I would not have my freedom of speech, my career, without you, and I am forever in your debt. The character of Pirate is an amalgamation of the warrior spirit I see in those who have returned home wounded. My heart extends to you, your families, and your caregivers—may you find comfort, peace, and healing as you go. Thank you.

Letter from the Author

Dear Reader,

Obviously my bias is toward organ and tissue donation. Maybe it's because of the health issues I've faced all my adult life, living with unrelenting pain, but I don't consider "me" attached to the body I'm in. If you want to call that my soul, or my energy—whatever you call it, I know that what makes me Amber isn't tied up in this broken body. When my body dies, I won't be here. To be honest, with my medical history, I don't know which, if any, of my pieces are useful—but I will leave that up to the experts to decide.

When I began this story, I knew who Jessica was immediately, but shortly thereafter, I met Vivian. From the beginning, I knew Vivian was a force of nature, received Jessica's heart and lungs, and dealt with the complicated and often overwhelming genetic disease cystic fibrosis.

There is a lot of medical information in this story, and to the best of my ability I've kept it as accurate as possible. I have greatly accelerated the time it takes for a person to heal and recover from an organ transplant. That can take months, if not years. I sped up the process to keep the story moving, not to minimize or diminish the journey. I also know that treatments, medications, and science are ever-changing fields and each body is different. That said, I made choices for these fictional patients that might be contrary to what you personally know or understand. I ask your forgiveness for mistakes and oversights.

As of 2012, the potential donations of one deceased person saved the lives of up to a dozen others and improved the quality of life for fifty more. That's an amazing amount of good that can come from a tragedy. Without organ donation the tragedy of one death is multiplied by at least two. There are many more people who need organs than those willing to donate them. And while great strides have been made on using living donors for organs like kidneys and livers, things like hearts, corneas, and tissue donations can only be used after death.

Give thought to whether you want to be an organ donor. There are many valid reasons to decide not to. But if you feel strongly one way or another, you need to have a conversation with your family. Consider a family plan. It's much easier to make decisions in a moment of crisis if everyone already knows their loved ones' wishes. This is a difficult conversation to start but often can elevate a family bond.

You can pledge to be an organ donor on your driver's license, at donatelife.org, and on Facebook.

For more information, visit:

United Network for Organ Sharing—unos.org

Children's Organ Transplant Association—cota.org

U.S. Government Information on Organ and Tissue Donation and Transplantation—organdonor.gov

American Transplant Foundation—americantransplantfoundation.org

What you need to know about cystic fibrosis

I knew in my gut Vivian had CF, but other than a vague idea that it was a disease that affects the lungs and the knowledge that those born with it die young, I had to start at the beginning. There is always an aspect of ser-endipity to my writing—maybe it hearkens back to how I started writing in the first place, but for whatever reason, serendipity is often what tells me I'm in the right place with the right story.

Cystic fibrosis is genetic. While it may affect more than one sibling in a family, it is not contagious. You cannot catch CF. At the most basic level, the cells in the body of a CF patient don't properly regulate water and salts. This thickens the mucus in the body, making it much harder, if not impossible, for the respiratory, gastrointestinal and digestive systems, and reproductive systems to function properly. CF is not a new disease—there are writings from the sixteenth century that talk about salty babies dying quickly. But in the last fifty years strides have been made in treatment and quality of life for those facing this disease.

As of 2013, the average life span of those diagnosed with CF is thirty-five to forty years. This is a huge improvement, but that's still less than midlife for most Americans. And like Vivian, those who have CF lose many friends and hospital mates. Educate yourself by checking out available resources at:

Cystic Fibrosis Foundation—cff.org

Boomer Esiason Foundation—esiason.org

The Breathing Room: The Art of Living with Cystic Fibrosis— thebreathingroom.org

What you need to know about liver diseases

The liver is the only organ in the human body that has the power to regenerate, which is why living donor transplants can be so successful. A portion of the donor's liver can be removed and it will grow back to its full function and size within both donor and recipient. There are genetic diseases that affect the liver, as well as viruses and cancer. The liver filters poisons outside the body, so alcohol, drugs, and toxins can also damage the liver, leading to failure. For more information, visit:

American Liver Foundation—liverfoundation.org

Columbia University Department of Surgery's Center for Liver Disease and Transplantation—LiverMD.org

What you need to know about kidney diseases

The kidneys have an important and complicated job in the human body. They remove waste from the blood, balance fluids in the body, help regulate blood pressure, and produce red blood cells. Kidney disease can be acute (right now!) or chronic (over a period of time). The main causes of kidney disease are congenital (born with), inherited from family, or diabetes and high blood pressure. Most people can function well with one kidney, which is why it's possible for living donors to give one kidney. African Americans, Pacific Islanders, and Hispanic Americans have a higher risk and incidence of kidney disease. Learn more at:

The National Kidney Foundation—kidney.org

About the Author

AMBER KIZER loves stories that wrestle with complicated choices, authentic emotion, and the unseen mysteries that connect us all. She is the author of seven young adult novels, including the Meridian books, *A Matter of Days*, and *Seven Kinds of Ordinary Catastrophes*. A rescued black Lab who sings "Happy Birthday"; adopted cats like Sugar, who carries pens like prey to Amber if she isn't working hard enough; and a flock of chickens who jump for bananas and enjoy chocolate cake keep things lively. Amber registered as a bone marrow donor and then as an organ donor as soon as she was allowed because saving lives doesn't require superpowers or a cape.

For more about Amber, please visit her at AmberKizer.com and send your thoughts to her at Amber@AmberKizer.com.